TOM SAWYER ABROAD

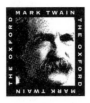

THE OXFORD MARK TWAIN

Shelley Fisher Fishkin, Editor

Tom Sawyer Abroad

Mark Twain

FOREWORD

SHELLEY FISHER FISHKIN

INTRODUCTION

NAT HENTOFF

AFTERWORD

M. THOMAS INGE

New York   Oxford

OXFORD UNIVERSITY PRESS

1996

OXFORD UNIVERSITY PRESS

Oxford   New York

Athens, Auckland, Bangkok, Bogotá, Bombay
Buenos Aires, Calcutta, Cape Town, Dar es Salaam
Delhi, Florence, Hong Kong, Istanbul, Karachi
Kuala Lumpur, Madras, Madrid, Melbourne
Mexico City, Nairobi, Paris, Singapore
Taipei, Tokyo, Toronto
and associated companies in
Berlin, Ibadan

Published by
Oxford University Press, Inc.
198 Madison Avenue, New York,
New York 10016

Oxford is a registered trademark of
Oxford University Press

Library of Congress
Cataloging-in-Publication Data

Twain, Mark, 1835–1910.
Tom Sawyer abroad / by Mark Twain; with an
introduction by Nat Hentoff and an afterword by
M. Thomas Inge.
p. cm. — (The Oxford Mark Twain)
Includes bibliographical references.
1. Sawyer, Tom (Fictitious character)—Fiction.
2. Americans—Travel—Foreign countries—Fiction.
3. Balloon ascensions—Fiction. I. Title. II. Series:
Twain, Mark. 1835–1910. Works. 1996.
PS1320.A1 1996
813'.4—dc20
96-16589
CIP
ISBN 0-19-510148-0 (trade ed.)
ISBN 0-19-511414-0 (lib. ed.)
ISBN 0-19-509088-8 (trade ed. set)
ISBN 0-19-511345-4 (lib. ed. set)

9 8 7 6 5 4 3 2 1

FRONTISPIECE

In this photograph, taken by James B. Pond aboard
the Man of War *Mohican*, Samuel L. Clemens is
dressed for his lecture at the Opera House in Seattle
in 1895, one year after *Tom Sawyer Abroad* was
published. (The Mark Twain House, Hartford,
Connecticut)

CONTENTS

EDITOR'S NOTE

The Oxford Mark Twain consists of twenty-nine volumes of facsimiles of the first American editions of Mark Twain's works, with an editor's foreword, new introductions, afterwords, notes on the texts, and essays on the illustrations in volumes with artwork. The facsimiles have been reproduced from the originals unaltered, except that blank pages in the front and back of the books have been omitted, and any seriously damaged or missing pages have been replaced by pages from other first editions (as indicated in the notes on the texts).

In the foreword, introduction, afterword, and essays on the illustrations, the titles of Mark Twain's works have been capitalized according to modern conventions, as have the names of characters (except where otherwise indicated). In the case of discrepancies between the title of a short story, essay, or sketch as it appears in the original table of contents and as it appears on its own title page, the title page has been followed. The parenthetical numbers in the introduction, afterwords, and illustration essays are page references to the facsimiles.

FOREWORD

Shelley Fisher Fishkin

Samuel Clemens entered the world and left it with Halley's Comet, little dreaming that generations hence Halley's Comet would be less famous than Mark Twain. He has been called the American Cervantes, our Homer, our Tolstoy, our Shakespeare, our Rabelais. Ernest Hemingway maintained that "all modern American literature comes from one book by Mark Twain called *Huckleberry Finn*." President Franklin Delano Roosevelt got the phrase "New Deal" from *A Connecticut Yankee in King Arthur's Court*. *The Gilded Age* gave an entire era its name. "The future historian of America," wrote George Bernard Shaw to Samuel Clemens, "will find your works as indispensable to him as a French historian finds the political tracts of Voltaire."[1]

There is a Mark Twain Bank in St. Louis, a Mark Twain Diner in Jackson Heights, New York, a Mark Twain Smoke Shop in Lakeland, Florida. There are Mark Twain Elementary Schools in Albuquerque, Dayton, Seattle, and Sioux Falls. Mark Twain's image peers at us from advertisements for Bass Ale (his drink of choice was Scotch), for a gas company in Tennessee, a hotel in the nation's capital, a cemetery in California.

Ubiquitous though his name and image may be, Mark Twain is in no danger of becoming a petrified icon. On the contrary: Mark Twain lives. *Huckleberry Finn* is "the most taught novel, most taught long work, and most taught piece of American literature" in American schools from junior high to the graduate level.[2] Hundreds of Twain impersonators appear in theaters, trade shows, and shopping centers in every region of the country.[3] Scholars publish hundreds of articles as well as books about Twain every year, and he is the subject of daily exchanges on the Internet. A journalist somewhere in the world finds a reason to quote Twain just about every day. Television series such as *Bonanza*, *Star Trek: The Next Generation*, and *Cheers* broadcast episodes that feature Mark Twain as a character. Hollywood screenwriters regularly produce movies inspired by his works, and writers of mysteries and science fiction continue to weave him into their plots.[4]

A century after the American Revolution sent shock waves throughout Europe, it took Mark Twain to explain to Europeans and to his countrymen alike what that revolution had wrought. He probed the significance of this new land and its new citizens, and identified what it was in the Old World that America abolished and rejected. The founding fathers had thought through the political dimensions of making a new society; Mark Twain took on the challenge of interpreting the social and cultural life of the United States for those outside its borders as well as for those who were living the changes he discerned.

Americans may have constructed a new society in the eighteenth century, but they articulated what they had done in voices that were largely inter-changeable with those of Englishmen until well into the nineteenth century. Mark Twain became the voice of the new land, the leading translator of what and who the "American" was — and, to a large extent, is. Frances Trollope's *Domestic Manners of the Americans,* a best-seller in England, Hector St. John de Crèvecoeur's *Letters from an American Farmer,* and Tocqueville's *Democracy in America* all tried to explain America to Europeans. But Twain did more than that: he allowed European readers to *experience* this strange "new world." And he gave his countrymen the tools to do two things they had not quite had the confidence to do before. He helped them stand before the cultural icons of the Old World unembarrassed, unashamed of America's lack of palaces and shrines, proud of its brash practicality and bold inventiveness, unafraid to reject European models of "civilization" as tainted or corrupt. And he also helped them recognize their own insularity, boorishness, arrogance, or ignorance, and laugh at it — the first step toward transcending it and becoming more "civilized," in the best European sense of the word.

Twain often strikes us as more a creature of our time than of his. He appreciated the importance and the complexity of mass tourism and public relations, fields that would come into their own in the twentieth century but were only fledgling enterprises in the nineteenth. He explored the liberating potential of humor and the dynamics of friendship, parenting, and marriage. He narrowed the gap between "popular" and "high" culture, and he meditated on the enigmas of personal and national identity. Indeed, it would be difficult to find an issue on the horizon today that Twain did not touch on somewhere in his work. Heredity versus environment? Animal rights? The boundaries of gender? The place of black voices in the cultural heritage of the United States? Twain was there.

With startling prescience and characteristic grace and wit, he zeroed in on many of the key challenges — political, social, and technological — that would face his country and the world for the next hundred years: the challenge of race relations in a society founded on both chattel slavery and ideals of equality, and the intractable problem of racism in American life; the potential of new technologies to transform our lives in ways that can be both exhilarating and terrifying — as well as unpredictable; the problem of imperialism and the difficulties entailed in getting rid of it. But he never lost sight of the most basic challenge of all: each man or woman's struggle for integrity in the face of the seductions of power, status, and material things.

Mark Twain's unerring sense of the right word and not its second cousin taught people to pay attention when he spoke, in person or in print. He said things that were smart and things that were wise, and he said them incomparably well. He defined the rhythms of our prose and the contours of our moral map. He saw our best and our worst, our extravagant promise and our stunning failures, our comic foibles and our tragic flaws. Throughout the world he is viewed as the most distinctively American of American authors — and as one of the most universal. He is assigned in classrooms in Naples, Riyadh, Belfast, and Beijing, and has been a major influence on twentieth-century writers from Argentina to Nigeria to Japan. The Oxford Mark Twain celebrates the versatility and vitality of this remarkable writer.

The Oxford Mark Twain reproduces the first American editions of Mark Twain's books published during his lifetime.[5] By encountering Twain's works in their original format — typography, layout, order of contents, and illustrations — readers today can come a few steps closer to the literary artifacts that entranced and excited readers when the books first appeared. Twain approved of and to a greater or lesser degree supervised the publication of all of this material.[6] The Mark Twain House in Hartford, Connecticut, generously loaned us its originals.[7] When more than one copy of a first American edition was available, Robert H. Hirst, general editor of the Mark Twain Project, in cooperation with Marianne Curling, curator of the Mark Twain House (and Jeffrey Kaimowitz, head of Rare Books for the Watkinson Library of Trinity College, Hartford, where the Mark Twain House collection is kept), guided our decision about which one to use.[8] As a set, the volumes also contain more than eighty essays commissioned especially for The Oxford Mark Twain, in which distinguished contributors reassess Twain's achievement as a writer and his place in the cultural conversation that he did so much to shape.

Each volume of The Oxford Mark Twain is introduced by a leading American, Canadian, or British writer who responds to Twain — often in a very personal way — as a fellow writer. Novelists, journalists, humorists, columnists, fabulists, poets, playwrights — these writers tell us what Twain taught them and what in his work continues to speak to them. Reading Twain's books, both famous and obscure, they reflect on the genesis of his art and the characteristics of his style, the themes he illuminated, and the aesthetic strategies he pioneered. Individually and collectively their contributions testify to the place Mark Twain holds in the hearts of readers of all kinds and temperaments.

Scholars whose work has shaped our view of Twain in the academy today have written afterwords to each volume, with suggestions for further reading. Their essays give us a sense of what was going on in Twain's life when he wrote the book at hand, and of how that book fits into his career. They explore how each book reflects and refracts contemporary events, and they show Twain responding to literary and social currents of the day, variously accepting, amplifying, modifying, and challenging prevailing paradigms. Sometimes they argue that works previously dismissed as quirky or eccentric departures actually address themes at the heart of Twain's work from the start. And as they bring new perspectives to Twain's composition strategies in familiar texts, several scholars see experiments in form where others saw only form-lessness, method where prior critics saw only madness. In addition to eluci-dating the work's historical and cultural context, the afterwords provide an overview of responses to each book from its first appearance to the present.

Most of Mark Twain's books involved more than Mark Twain's words: unique illustrations. The parodic visual send-ups of "high culture" that Twain himself drew for *A Tramp Abroad*, the sketch of financial manipulator Jay Gould as a greedy and sadistic "Slave Driver" in *A Connecticut Yankee in King Arthur's Court*, and the memorable drawings of Eve in *Eve's Diary* all helped Twain's books to be sold, read, discussed, and preserved. In their es-says for each volume that contains artwork, Beverly R. David and Ray Sapirstein highlight the significance of the sketches, engravings, and pho-tographs in the first American editions of Mark Twain's works, and tell us what is known about the public response to them.

The Oxford Mark Twain invites us to read some relatively neglected works by Twain in the company of some of the most engaging literary figures of our time. Roy Blount Jr., for example, riffs in a deliciously Twain-like manner on "An Item Which the Editor Himself Could Not Understand," which may well rank as one of the least-known pieces Twain ever published. Bobbie Ann Mason celebrates the "mad energy" of Twain's most obscure comic novel, *The American Claimant*, in which the humor "hurtles beyond tall tale into simon-pure absurdity."[9] Garry Wills finds that *Christian Science* "gets us very close to the heart of American culture." Lee Smith reads "Political Economy" as a sharp and funny essay on language. Walter Mosley sees "The Stolen White Elephant," a story "reduced to a series of ridiculous telegrams related by an untrustworthy narrator caught up in an adventure that is as impossible as it is ludicrous," as a stunningly compact and economical satire of a world we still recognize as our own. Anne Bernays returns to "The Private History of a Campaign That Failed" and finds "an antiwar manifesto that is also confession, dramatic monologue, a plea for understanding and absolution, and a romp that gradually turns into atrocity even as we watch." After revisiting Captain Stormfield's heaven, Frederik Pohl finds that there "is no imaginable place more pleasant to spend eternity." Indeed, Pohl writes, "one would almost be willing to die to enter it."

While less familiar works receive fresh attention in The Oxford Mark Twain, new light is cast on the best-known works as well. Judith Martin ("Miss Manners") points out that it is by reading a court etiquette book that Twain's pauper learns how to behave as a proper prince. As important as etiquette may be in the palace, Martin notes, it is even more important in the slums.

> That etiquette is a sorer point with the ruffians in the street than with the proud dignitaries of the prince's court may surprise some readers. As in our own streets, etiquette is always a more volatile subject among those who cannot count on being treated with respect than among those who have the power to command deference.

And taking a fresh look at *Adventures of Huckleberry Finn,* Toni Morrison writes,

> much of the novel's genius lies in its quiescence, the silences that pervade it and give it a porous quality that is by turns brooding and soothing. It lies in . . . the subdued images in which the repetition of a simple word, such as "lonesome," tolls like an evening bell; the moments when nothing is said, when scenes and incidents swell the heart unbearably precisely because unarticulated, and force an act of imagination almost against the will.

Engaging Mark Twain as one writer to another, several contributors to The Oxford Mark Twain offer new insights into the processes by which his books came to be. Russell Banks, for example, reads *A Tramp Abroad* as "an important revision of Twain's incomplete first draft of *Huckleberry Finn,* a second draft, if you will, which in turn made possible the third and final draft." Erica Jong suggests that *1601,* a freewheeling parody of Elizabethan manners and mores, written during the same summer Twain began *Huckleberry Finn*, served as "a warm-up for his creative process" and "primed the pump for other sorts of freedom of expression." And Justin Kaplan suggests that "one of the transcendent figures standing behind and shaping" *Joan of Arc* was Ulysses S. Grant, whose memoirs Twain had recently published, and who, like Joan, had risen unpredictably "from humble and obscure origins" to become a "military genius" endowed with "the gift of command, a natural eloquence, and an equally natural reserve."

As a number of contributors note, Twain was a man ahead of his times. *The Gilded Age* was the first "Washington novel," Ward Just tells us, because "Twain was the first to see the possibilities that had eluded so many others." Commenting on *The Tragedy of Pudd'nhead Wilson*, Sherley Anne Williams observes that "Twain's argument about the power of environment in shaping character runs directly counter to prevailing sentiment where the negro was concerned." Twain's fictional technology, wildly fanciful by the standards of his day, predicts developments we take for granted in ours. DNA cloning, fax machines, and photocopiers are all prefigured, Bobbie Ann Mason tells us, in *The American Claimant*. Cynthia Ozick points out that the "telelectrophonoscope" we meet in "From the 'London Times' of 1904" is suspiciously like what we know as "television." And Malcolm Bradbury suggests that in the "phrenophones" of "Mental Telegraphy" "the Internet was born."

Twain turns out to have been remarkably prescient about political affairs as well. Kurt Vonnegut sees in *A Connecticut Yankee* a chilling foreshadowing (or perhaps a projection from the Civil War) of "all the high-tech atrocities which followed, and which follow still." Cynthia Ozick suggests that "The Man That Corrupted Hadleyburg," along with some of the other pieces collected under that title — many of them written when Twain lived in a Vienna ruled by Karl Lueger, a demagogue Adolf Hitler would later idolize — shoot up moral flares that shed an eerie light on the insidious corruption, prejudice, and hatred that reached bitter fruition under the Third Reich. And Twain's portrait in this book of "the dissolving Austria-Hungary of the 1890s," in Ozick's view, presages not only the Sarajevo that would erupt in 1914 but also "the disintegrated components of the former Yugoslavia" and "the *fin-de-siècle* Sarajevo of our own moment."

Despite their admiration for Twain's ambitious reach and scope, contributors to The Oxford Mark Twain also recognize his limitations. Mordecai Richler, for example, thinks that "the early pages of *Innocents Abroad* suffer from being a tad broad, proffering more burlesque than inspired satire," perhaps because Twain was "trying too hard for knee-slappers." Charles Johnson notes that the Young Man in Twain's philosophical dialogue about free will and determinism (*What Is Man?*) "caves in far too soon," failing to challenge what through late-twentieth-century eyes looks like "pseudoscience" and suspect essentialism in the Old Man's arguments.

Some contributors revisit their first encounters with Twain's works, recalling what surprised or intrigued them. When David Bradley came across "Fenimore Cooper's Literary Offences" in his college library, he "did not at first realize that Twain was being his usual ironic self with all this business about the 'nineteen rules governing literary art in the domain of romantic fiction,' but by the time I figured out there was no such list outside Twain's own head, I had decided that the rules made *sense.* . . . It seemed to me they were a pretty good blueprint for writing — Negro writing included." Sherley Anne Williams remembers that part of what attracted her to *Pudd'nhead Wilson* when she first read it thirty years ago was "that Twain, writing at the end of the nineteenth century, could imagine negroes as characters, albeit white ones, who actually thought for and of themselves, whose actions were the product of their thinking rather than the spontaneous ephemera of physical instincts that stereotype assigned to blacks." Frederik Pohl recalls his first reading of *Huckleberry Finn* as "a watershed event" in his life, the first book he read as a child in which "bad people" ceased to exercise a monopoly on doing "bad things." In *Huckleberry Finn* "some seriously bad things — things like the possession and mistreatment of black slaves, like stealing and lying, even like killing other people in duels — were quite often done by people who not only thought of themselves as exemplarily moral but, by any other standards I knew how to apply, actually *were* admirable citizens." The world that

Tom and Huck lived in, Pohl writes, "was filled with complexities and contradictions," and resembled "the world I appeared to be living in myself."

Other contributors explore their more recent encounters with Twain, explaining why they have revised their initial responses to his work. For Toni Morrison, parts of *Huckleberry Finn* that she "once took to be deliberate evasions, stumbles even, or a writer's impatience with his or her material," now strike her "as otherwise: as entrances, crevices, gaps, seductive invitations flashing the possibility of meaning. Unarticulated eddies that encourage diving into the novel's undertow — the real place where writer captures reader." One such "eddy" is the imprisonment of Jim on the Phelps farm. Instead of dismissing this portion of the book as authorial bungling, as she once did, Morrison now reads it as Twain's commentary on the 1880s, a period that "saw the collapse of civil rights for blacks," a time when "the nation, as well as Tom Sawyer, was deferring Jim's freedom in agonizing play." Morrison believes that Americans in the 1880s were attempting "to bury the combustible issues Twain raised in his novel," and that those who try to kick Huck Finn out of school in the 1990s are doing the same: "The cyclical attempts to remove the novel from classrooms extend Jim's captivity on into each generation of readers."

Although imitation-Hemingway and imitation-Faulkner writing contests draw hundreds of entries annually, no one has ever tried to mount a faux-Twain competition. Why? Perhaps because Mark Twain's voice is too much a part of who we are and how we speak even today. Roy Blount Jr. suggests that it is impossible, "at least for an American writer, to parody Mark Twain. It would be like doing an impression of your father or mother: he or she is already there in your voice."

Twain's style is examined and celebrated in The Oxford Mark Twain by fellow writers who themselves have struggled with the nuances of words, the structure of sentences, the subtleties of point of view, and the trickiness of opening lines. Bobbie Ann Mason observes, for example, that "Twain loved the sound of words and he knew how to string them by sound, like different shades of one color: 'The earl's barbaric eye,' 'the Usurping Earl,' 'a double-dyed humbug.'" Twain "relied on the punch of plain words" to show writers how to move beyond the "wordy romantic rubbish" so prevalent in nineteenth-century fiction, Mason says; he "was one of the first writers in America to deflower literary language." Lee Smith believes that "American writers have benefited as much from the way Mark Twain opened up the possibilities of first-person narration as we have from his use of vernacular language." (She feels that "the ghost of Mark Twain was hovering someplace in the background" when she decided to write her novel *Oral History* from the standpoint of multiple first-person narrators.) Frederick Busch maintains that "A Dog's Tale" "boasts one of the great opening sentences" of all time: "My father was a St. Bernard, my mother was a collie, but I am a Presbyterian." And Ursula Le Guin marvels at the ingenuity of the following sentence that she encounters in *Extracts from Adam's Diary.*

> . . . This made her sorry for the creatures which live in there, which she calls fish, for she continues to fasten names on to things that don't need them and don't come when they are called by them, which is a matter of no consequence to her, as she is such a numskull anyway; so she got a lot of them out and brought them in last night and put them in my bed to keep warm, but I have noticed them now and then all day, and I don't see that they are any happier there than they were before, only quieter.[10]

Le Guin responds,

> Now, that is a pure Mark-Twain-tour-de-force sentence, covering an immense amount of territory in an effortless, aimless ramble that seems to be heading nowhere in particular and ends up with breathtaking accuracy at the gold mine. Any sensible child would find that funny, perhaps not following all its divagations but delighted by the swing of it, by the word "numskull," by the idea of putting fish in the bed; and as that child grew older and reread it, its reward would only grow; and if that grown-up child had to write an essay on the piece and therefore earnestly studied and pored over this sentence, she would end up in unmitigated admiration of its vocabulary, syntax, pacing, sense, and rhythm, above all the beautiful

timing of the last two words; and she would, and she does, still find it funny.

The fish surface again in a passage that Gore Vidal calls to our attention, from *Following the Equator*: "'The Whites always mean well when they take human fish out of the ocean and try to make them dry and warm and happy and comfortable in a chicken coop,' which is how, through civilization, they did away with many of the original inhabitants. Lack of empathy is a principal theme in Twain's meditations on race and empire."

Indeed, empathy — and its lack — is a principal theme in virtually all of Twain's work, as contributors frequently note. Nat Hentoff quotes the following thoughts from Huck in *Tom Sawyer Abroad*:

> I see a bird setting on a dead limb of a high tree, singing with its head tilt-ed back and its mouth open, and before I thought I fired, and his song stopped and he fell straight down from the limb, all limp like a rag, and I run and picked him up and he was dead, and his body was warm in my hand, and his head rolled about this way and that, like his neck was broke, and there was a little white skin over his eyes, and one little drop of blood on the side of his head; and laws! I could n't see nothing more for the tears; and I hain't never murdered no creature since that war n't doing me no harm, and I ain't going to.[11]

"The Humane Society," Hentoff writes, "has yet to say anything as powerful — and lasting."

Readers of The Oxford Mark Twain will have the pleasure of revisiting Twain's Mississippi landmarks alongside Willie Morris, whose own lower Mississippi Valley boyhood gives him a special sense of connection to Twain. Morris knows firsthand the mosquitoes described in *Life on the Mississippi* — so colossal that "two of them could whip a dog" and "four of them could hold a man down"; in Morris's own hometown they were so large during the flood season that "local wags said they wore wristwatches." Morris's Yazoo City and Twain's Hannibal shared a "rough-hewn democracy . . . complicated by all the visible textures of caste and class, . . . harmless boyhood fun and mischief right along with . . . rank hypocrisies, churchgoing sanctimonies, racial hatred, entrenched and unrepentant greed."

For the West of Mark Twain's *Roughing It*, readers will have George Plimpton as their guide. "What a group these newspapermen were!" Plimpton writes about Twain and his friends Dan De Quille and Joe Goodman in Virginia City, Nevada. "Their roisterous carryings-on bring to mind the kind of frat-house enthusiasm one associates with college humor magazines like the *Harvard Lampoon*." Malcolm Bradbury examines Twain as "a living example of what made the American so different from the European." And Hal Holbrook, who has interpreted Mark Twain on stage for some forty years, describes how Twain "played" during the civil rights movement, during the Vietnam War, during the Gulf War, and in Prague on the eve of the demise of Communism.

Why do we continue to read Mark Twain? What draws us to him? His wit? His compassion? His humor? His bravura? His humility? His understanding of who and what we are in those parts of our being that we rarely open to view? Our sense that he knows we can do better than we do? Our sense that he knows we can't? E. L. Doctorow tells us that children are attracted to *Tom Sawyer* because in this book "the young reader confirms his own hope that no matter how troubled his relations with his elders may be, beneath all their disapproval is their underlying love for him, constant and steadfast." Readers in general, Arthur Miller writes, value Twain's "insights into America's always uncertain moral life and its shifting but everlasting hypocrisies"; we appreciate the fact that he "is not using his alienation from the public illusions of his hour in order to reject the country implicitly as though he could live without it, but manifestly in order to correct it." Perhaps we keep reading Mark Twain because, in Miller's words, he "wrote much more like a father than a son. He doesn't seem to be sitting in class taunting the teacher but standing at the head of it challenging his students to acknowledge their own humanity, that is, their immemorial attraction to the untrue."

Mark Twain entered the public eye at a time when many of his countrymen considered "American culture" an oxymoron; he died four years before a world conflagration that would lead many to question whether the contradiction in terms was not "European civilization" instead. In between he worked in journalism, printing, steamboating, mining, lecturing, publishing, and editing, in virtually every region of the country. He tried his hand at humorous sketches, social satire, historical novels, children's books, poetry, drama, science fiction, mysteries, romance, philosophy, travelogue, memoir, polemic, and several genres no one had ever seen before or has ever seen since. He invented a self-pasting scrapbook, a history game, a vest strap, and a gizmo for keeping bed sheets tucked in; he invested in machines and processes designed to revolutionize typesetting and engraving, and in a food supplement called "Plasmon." Along the way he cheerfully impersonated himself and prior versions of himself for doting publics on five continents while playing out a charming rags-to-riches story followed by a devastating riches-to-rags story followed by yet another great American comeback. He had a long-running real-life engagement in a sumptuous comedy of manners, and then in a real-life tragedy not of his own design: during the last fourteen years of his life almost everyone he ever loved was taken from him by disease and death.

Mark Twain has indelibly shaped our views of who and what the United States is as a nation and of who and what we might become. He understood the nostalgia for a "simpler" past that increased as that past receded — and he saw through the nostalgia to a past that was just as complex as the present. He recognized better than we did ourselves our potential for greatness and our potential for disaster. His fictions brilliantly illuminated the world in which he lived, changing it — and us — in the process. He knew that our feet often danced to tunes that had somehow remained beyond our hearing; with perfect pitch he played them back to us.

My mother read *Tom Sawyer* to me as a bedtime story when I was eleven. I thought Huck and Tom could be a lot of fun, but I dismissed Becky Thatcher as a bore. When I was twelve I invested a nickel at a local garage sale in a book that contained short pieces by Mark Twain. That was where I met Twain's Eve. Now, *that's* more like it, I decided, pleased to meet a female character I could identify *with* instead of against. Eve had spunk. Even if she got a lot wrong, you had to give her credit for trying. "The Man That Corrupted

Hadleyburg" left me giddy with satisfaction: none of my adolescent reveries of getting even with my enemies were half as neat as the plot of the man who got back at that town. "How I Edited an Agricultural Paper" set me off in uncontrollable giggles.

People sometimes told me that I looked like Huck Finn. "It's the freckles," they'd explain — not explaining anything at all. I didn't read *Huckleberry Finn* until junior year in high school in my English class. It was the fall of 1965. I was living in a small town in Connecticut. I expected a sequel to *Tom Sawyer*. So when the teacher handed out the books and announced our assignment, my jaw dropped: "Write a paper on how Mark Twain used irony to attack racism in *Huckleberry Finn*."

The year before, the bodies of three young men who had gone to Mississippi to help blacks register to vote — James Chaney, Andrew Goodman, and Michael Schwerner — had been found in a shallow grave; a group of white segregationists (the county sheriff among them) had been arrested in connection with the murders. America's inner cities were simmering with pent-up rage that began to explode in the summer of 1965, when riots in Watts left thirty-four people dead. None of this made any sense to me. I was confused, angry, certain that there was something missing from the news stories I read each day: the why. Then I met Pap Finn. And the Phelpses.

Pap Finn, Huck tells us, "had been drunk over in town" and "was just all mud." He erupts into a drunken tirade about "a free nigger . . . from Ohio — a mulatter, most as white as a white man," with "the whitest shirt on you ever see, too, and the shiniest hat; and there ain't a man in town that's got as fine clothes as what he had."

> . . . they said he was a p'fessor in a college, and could talk all kinds of languages, and knowed everything. And that ain't the wust. They said he could *vote*, when he was at home. Well, that let me out. Thinks I, what is the country a-coming to? It was 'lection day, and I was just about to go and vote, myself, if I warn't too drunk to get there; but when they told me there was a State in this country where they'd let that nigger vote, I drawed out. I says I'll never vote agin. Them's the very words I said. . . . And to see the

cool way of that nigger — why, he wouldn't a give me the road if I hadn't shoved him out o' the way.[12]

Later on in the novel, when the runaway slave Jim gives up his freedom to nurse a wounded Tom Sawyer, a white doctor testifies to the stunning altruism of his actions. The Phelpses and their neighbors, all fine, upstanding, well-meaning, churchgoing folk,

> agreed that Jim had acted very well, and was deserving to have some notice took of it, and reward. So every one of them promised, right out and hearty, that they wouldn't curse him no more.
>
> Then they come out and locked him up. I hoped they was going to say he could have one or two of the chains took off, because they was rotten heavy, or could have meat and greens with his bread and water, but they didn't think of it.[13]

Why did the behavior of these people tell me more about why Watts burned than anything I had read in the daily paper? And why did a drunk Pap Finn railing against a black college professor from Ohio whose vote was as good as his own tell me more about white anxiety over black political power than anything I had seen on the evening news?

Mark Twain knew that there was nothing, absolutely *nothing*, a black man could do — including selflessly sacrificing his freedom, the only thing of value he had — that would make white society see beyond the color of his skin. And Mark Twain knew that depicting racists with chilling accuracy would expose the viciousness of their world view like nothing else could. It was an insight echoed some eighty years after Mark Twain penned Pap Finn's rantings about the black professor, when Malcolm X famously asked, "Do you know what white racists call black Ph.D.'s?" and answered, "'*Nigger!*'"[14]

Mark Twain taught me things I needed to know. He taught me to understand the raw racism that lay behind what I saw on the evening news. He taught me that the most well-meaning people can be hurtful and myopic. He taught me to recognize the supreme irony of a country founded in freedom that continued to deny freedom to so many of its citizens. Every time I hear of another effort to kick Huck Finn out of school somewhere, I recall everything that Mark Twain taught *this* high school junior, and I find myself jumping into the fray.[15] I remember the black high school student who called CNN during the phone-in portion of a 1985 debate between Dr. John Wallace, a black educator spearheading efforts to ban the book, and myself. She accused Dr. Wallace of insulting her and all black high school students by suggesting they weren't smart enough to understand Mark Twain's irony. And I recall the black cameraman on the *CBS Morning News* who came up to me after he finished shooting another debate between Dr. Wallace and myself. He said he had never read the book by Mark Twain that we had been arguing about — but now he really wanted to. One thing that puzzled him, though, was why a white woman was defending it and a black man was attacking it, because as far as he could see from what we'd been saying, the book made whites look pretty bad.

As I came to understand *Huckleberry Finn* and *Pudd'nhead Wilson* as commentaries on the era now known as the nadir of American race relations, those books pointed me toward the world recorded in nineteenth-century black newspapers and periodicals and in fiction by Mark Twain's black contemporaries. My investigation of the role black voices and traditions played in shaping Mark Twain's art helped make me aware of their role in shaping all of American culture.[16] My research underlined for me the importance of changing the stories we tell about who we are to reflect the realities of what we've been.[17]

Ever since our encounter in high school English, Mark Twain has shown me the potential of American literature and American history to illuminate each other. Rarely have I found a contradiction or complexity we grapple with as a nation that Mark Twain had not puzzled over as well. He insisted on taking America seriously. And he insisted on *not* taking America seriously: "I think that there is but a single specialty with us, only one thing that can be called by the wide name 'American,'" he once wrote. "That is the national devotion to ice-water."[18]

Mark Twain threw back at us our dreams and our denial of those dreams, our greed, our goodness, our ambition, and our laziness, all rattling around together in that vast echo chamber of our talk — that sharp, spunky American talk that Mark Twain figured out how to write down without robbing it of its energy and immediacy. Talk shaped by voices that the official arbiters of "culture" deemed of no importance — voices of children, voices of slaves, voices of servants, voices of ordinary people. Mark Twain listened. And he made us listen. To the stories he told us, and to the truths they conveyed. He still has a lot to say that we need to hear.

Mark Twain lives — in our libraries, classrooms, homes, theaters, movie houses, streets, and most of all in our speech. His optimism energizes us, his despair sobers us, and his willingness to keep wrestling with the hilarious and horrendous complexities of it all keeps us coming back for more. As the twenty-first century approaches, may he continue to goad us, chasten us, delight us, berate us, and cause us to erupt in unrestrained laughter in unexpected places.

NOTES

1. Ernest Hemingway, *Green Hills of Africa* (New York: Charles Scribner's Sons, 1935), 22. George Bernard Shaw to Samuel L. Clemens, July 3, 1907, quoted in Albert Bigelow Paine, *Mark Twain: A Biography* (New York: Harper and Brothers, 1912), 3:1398.

2. Allen Carey-Webb, "Racism and *Huckleberry Finn*: Censorship, Dialogue and Change," *English Journal* 82, no. 7 (November 1993):22.

3. See Louis J. Budd, "Impersonators," in J. R. LeMaster and James D. Wilson, eds., *The Mark Twain Encyclopedia* (New York: Garland Publishing Company, 1993), 389–91.

4. See Shelley Fisher Fishkin, "Ripples and Reverberations," part 3 of *Lighting Out for the Territory: Reflections on Mark Twain and American Culture* (New York: Oxford University Press, 1996).

5. There are two exceptions. Twain published chapters from his autobiography in the *North American Review* in 1906 and 1907, but this material was not published in book form in Twain's lifetime; our volume reproduces the material as it appeared in the *North American Review*. The other exception is our final volume, *Mark Twain's Speeches*, which appeared two months after Twain's death in 1910.

An unauthorized handful of copies of *1601* was privately printed by an Alexander Gunn of Cleveland at the instigation of Twain's friend John Hay in 1880. The first American edition authorized by Mark Twain, however, was printed at the United States Military Academy at West Point in 1882; that is the edition reproduced here.

It should further be noted that four volumes — *The Stolen White Elephant and Other Detective Stories, Following the Equator and Anti-imperialist Essays, The Diaries of Adam and Eve,* and *1601, and Is Shakespeare Dead?* — bind together material originally published separately. In each case the first American edition of the material is the version that has been reproduced, always in its entirety. Because Twain constantly recycled and repackaged previously published works in his collections of short pieces, a certain amount of duplication is unavoidable. We have selected volumes with an eye toward keeping this duplication to a minimum.

Even the twenty-nine-volume Oxford Mark Twain has had to leave much out. No edition of Twain can ever claim to be "complete," for the man was too prolix, and the file drawers of both ephemera and as yet unpublished texts are deep.

6. With the possible exception of *Mark Twain's Speeches*. Some scholars suspect Twain knew about this book and may have helped shape it, although no hard evidence to that effect has yet surfaced. Twain's involvement in the production process varied greatly from book to book. For a fuller sense of authorial intention, scholars will continue to rely on the superb definitive editions of Twain's works produced by the Mark Twain Project at the University of California at Berkeley as they become available. Dense with annotation documenting textual emendation and related issues, these editions add immeasurably to our understanding of Mark Twain and the genesis of his works.

7. Except for a few titles that were not in its collection. The American Antiquarian Society in Worcester, Massachusetts, provided the first edition of *King Leopold's Soliloquy*; the Elmer Holmes Bobst Library of New York University furnished the 1906–7 volumes of the *North American Review* in which *Chapters from My Autobiography* first appeared; the Harry Ransom Humanities Research Center at the University of Texas at Austin made their copy of the West Point edition of *1601* available; and the Mark Twain Project provided the first edition of *Extract from Captain Stormfield's Visit to Heaven*.

8. The specific copy photographed for Oxford's facsimile edition is indicated in a note on the text at the end of each volume.

9. All quotations from contemporary writers in this essay are taken from their introductions to the volumes of The Oxford Mark Twain, and the quotations from Mark Twain's works are taken from the texts reproduced in The Oxford Mark Twain.

10. *The Diaries of Adam and Eve*, The Oxford Mark Twain [hereafter OMT] (New York: Oxford University Press, 1996), p. 33.

11. *Tom Sawyer Abroad*, OMT, p. 74.

12. *Adventures of Huckleberry Finn*, OMT, p. 49–50.

13. Ibid., p. 358.

14. Malcolm X, *The Autobiography of Malcolm X*, with the assistance of Alex Haley (New York: Grove Press, 1965), p. 284.

15. I do not mean to minimize the challenge of teaching this difficult novel, a challenge for which all teachers may not feel themselves prepared. Elsewhere I have developed some concrete strategies for approaching the book in the classroom, including teaching it in the context of the history of American race relations and alongside books by black writers. See Shelley Fisher Fishkin, "Teaching *Huckleberry Finn,*" in James S. Leonard, ed., *Making Mark Twain Work in the Classroom* (Durham: Duke University Press, forthcoming). See also Shelley Fisher Fishkin, *Was Huck Black? Mark Twain and African-American Voices* (New York: Oxford University Press, 1993), pp. 106–8, and a curriculum kit in preparation at the Mark Twain House in Hartford, containing teaching suggestions from myself, David Bradley, Jocelyn Chadwick-Joshua, James Miller, and David E. E. Sloane.

16. See Fishkin, *Was Huck Black?* See also Fishkin, "Interrogating 'Whiteness,' Complicating 'Blackness': Remapping American Culture," in Henry Wonham, ed., *Criticism and the Color Line: Desegregating American Literary Studies* (New Brunswick: Rutgers UP, 1996, pp. 251–90 and in shortened form in *American Quarterly* 47, no. 3 (September 1995):428–66.

17. I explore the roots of my interest in Mark Twain and race at greater length in an essay entitled "Changing the Story," in Jeffrey Rubin-Dorsky and Shelley Fisher Fishkin, eds., *People of the Book: Thirty Scholars Reflect on Their Jewish Identity* (Madison: U of Wisconsin Press, 1996), pp. 47–63.

18. "What Paul Bourget Thinks of Us," *How to Tell a Story and Other Essays*, OMT, p. 197.

INTRODUCTION

Nat Hentoff

The key to *Tom Sawyer Abroad* has been provided by the author: "I conceive that the right way to write a story for boys is to write so that it will not only interest boys but will strongly interest *any man who has ever been a boy.*"
This novel is clearly a story for boys. Not all men remember being boys, but those who do will be able to go back in time to the wondrous surprises in books that transported them beyond their neighborhoods and cities and countries to lands and experiences they could not have imagined before.

Although the river in *Adventures of Huckleberry Finn* has become the boundless sky in *Tom Sawyer Abroad*, it was the Mississippi that coursed through Twain's memories of boyhood which very much stayed with him until the end.

In "Old Times on the Mississippi," he wrote, "When I was a boy, there was but one permanent ambition among my comrades in our village [Hannibal] on the west bank of the Mississippi River. That was to be a steamboatman." He dreamed of being a pilot; but on the way he became a passenger on a journey that he thought would take him to South America to "complete the exploration of the Amazon."

"I was a traveler! . . . I had an exultant sense of being bound for mysterious lands and distant climes. . . . I was able to look down and pity the untraveled. . . .

. . . . I wished that the boys and girls at home could see me now.

Tom Sawyer Abroad was written in the hope and desire that it would be part of a series in which the adventurers would explore the dangers and rewards of charted and uncharted lands. The aim, of course, was to increase sales, but the writing indicates that Twain enjoyed renewing the boyhood memory of the "exultant sense of being bound for mysterious lands." In an August 1892 letter to Fred J. Hall, manager of Twain's publishing firm, Charles L. Webster and Company, Twain announced, "So I have started Huck Finn and Tom Sawyer (still 15 years old) and their friend the freed slave Jim around the world in a stray balloon, with Huck as narrator."

The novel has been criticized as being insufficiently funny, but Twain was more interested in creating an atmosphere of the best kind of exhilarating adventures for boys — scary events and scarier assaults from wholly uncontrollable natural forces.

> All around us was a ring, where the sky and the water come together; yes, a monstrous big ring it was, and we right in the dead center of it — plumb in the center. We was racing along like a prairie fire, but it never made any difference, we could n't seem to git past that center no way. I couldn't see that we ever gained an inch on that ring. It made a body feel creepy, it was so curious and unaccountable. (56)

For the traveler in imagination — boy and man, girl and woman — a particular vicarious pleasure is reading about fear.

> It was dreadful the way the thunder boomed and tore, and the lightning glared out, and the wind sung and screamed in the rigging, and the rain come down. One second you could n't see your hand before you, and the next you could count the threads in your coat-sleeve. (65)

Twain also goes back to one of the abiding pleasures of boyhood: doing nothing. Sailing over the "solemn, peaceful desert. . . we had cramped the speed down . . . and was having a most noble good lazy time," Huck says.

> Always I had had hateful people around me, a-nagging at me, and pester-

ing of me, and scolding, and finding fault, and fussing and bothering, and sticking to me, and keeping after me, and making me do this, and making me do that and t'other, and always selecting out the things I did n't want to do, and then giving me Sam Hill because I shirked and done something else, and just aggravating the life out of a body all the time; but up here in the sky it was so still and sun-shiny and lovely, and plenty to eat, and plenty of sleep, and strange things to see, and no nagging and pestering, and no good people, and just holiday all the time. Land, I war n't in no hurry to git out and buck at civilization again. (106–09)

Whether in the nineteenth, twentieth or twenty-first century, that passage is likely to delight — as the ringmaster in the circus says — children of all ages, all over the world. To be sure, there are no laughs in it, but there's a good deal more to Mark Twain, of course, than laughs.

There are also no laughs in the corpses the travelers come upon in the desert — victims, they later find out, of a sandstorm: "There was men, and women, and children. They was dried by the sun and dark and shriveled and leathery, like the pictures of mummies you see in books. And yet they looked . . . just like they was asleep" (117).

A man was setting with his hands locked around his knees, staring out of his dead eyes at a young girl that was stretched out before him. He looked so mournful, it was pitiful to see. And you never see a place so still as that was. He had straight black hair hanging down by his cheeks, and when a little faint breeze fanned it and made it wag, it made me shudder, because it seemed as if he was wagging his head. . . .

When we was going to put sand on her, the man's hair wagged again and give us a shock, and we stopped, because it looked like he was trying to tell us he didn't want her covered up so he couldn't see her no more. I reckon she was dear to him, and he would a been so lonesome.

That passage, which is seldom quoted from *Tom Sawyer Abroad* (it was one of many deleted by Mary Mapes Dodge, editor of the children's magazine *St.*

Nicholas, when she serialized the novel), underscores, as Thomas Inge points out in his afterword to this volume, how frequently this narrative deals with death.

The encounter with the corpses is one of many episodes that reveal the disparate ways in which Tom, Huck, and Jim look at the world, and at themselves. Tom is the house intellectual on the balloon, impatient at what he considers his colleagues' inferior command of logic. Yet Tom can be considerably more parochial than he realizes. For example, when they see the whirling dervishes in Cairo and Huck asks Tom what a Moslem is, Tom says readily that a Moslem is a person who isn't a Presbyterian.

Huck is not nearly so challenged in soul and tradition as he is in *Adventures of Huckleberry Finn*, but he remains an engaging teenager with none of the occasional portentousness of Tom. Remarkably and consistently observant, Huck may not fully understand everything he sees, but he does not pretend to. Accordingly, he is ceaselessly, infectiously curious. As in *Adventures of Huckleberry Finn*, there is also a tenderness in Huck that is one of the many reasons that novel — and this one, too — should be in the curriculums of secondary schools. In America, at any rate, we are moving into an ice age toward those who are vulnerable — human and animal.

For further illustration of the dimensions of this novel, there are no laughs, either, in Huck's memory of the day he hunted a bird:

> I see a bird setting on a limb of a high tree, singing with its head tilted back and its mouth open, and before I thought I fired, and his song stopped and he fell straight down from the limb, all limp like a rag, and I run and picked him up and he was dead, and his body was warm in my hand, and his head rolled about this way and that, like his neck was broke, and there was a little white skin over his eyes, and one little drop of blood on the side of his head; and laws! I could n't see nothing more for the tears; and I hain't never murdered no creature since that war n't doing me no harm, and I ain't going to. (74)

The Humane Society has yet to say anything as powerful — and lasting.

Jim is not primary focus of Mark Twain's concern in *Tom Sawyer Abroad*. For the most part, he is one-dimensional, predictable, and not particularly interesting. Jim often displays strength and wisdom in *Adventures of Huckleberry Finn*, but here, except in a few pages, he could have been played by Stepin Fetchit. In passing, Huck Finn says about Jim, "He was only a nigger outside; inside he was as white as you be."(182) It is as if Mark Twain, troubled by the stereotypes he has made of Jim, wants to appease his conscience.

The novel is most compelling and dramatic when it returns to the sorts of bold adventures of which boys daydream. Watching the end of an attack on a caravan, the travelers in the sky see a brigand on horseback snatch up a child and carry it away "and a woman run screaming and begging after him, and followed him away off across the plain till she was separated a long ways from her people; but it wan't no use, and she had to give it up, and we see her sink down on the sand and cover her face with her hands" (93–94). Tom Sawyer swoops down and knocks the villain — and the child — off the horse, but the child is unhurt, "working its hands and legs in the air like a tumble-bug that's on its back and can't turn over." Whereupon Jim, going down the ladder, fetches "the nice fat little thing," and then deposits the child with its mother.

As that adventure ends, Twain presciently provides an image that could go straight into a movie scenario: "In a minute we was back up in the sky and the woman was staring up, with the back of her head between her shoulders and the child with its arms locked around her neck. And there she stood, as long as we was in sight a-sailing away in the sky."

Unlike some spinners of tales for boys, Twain did not leave his narrative a-sailing away in the sky. Jim, having been sent back home in the balloon to get Tom's pipe, returns with the weight of the world on him: that is, a message from she who must be obeyed, Aunt Polly. "Mars Tom, she's out on de porch wid her eye sot on de sky a-layin' for you, en she say she ain't gwyne to budge from dah tell she gits hold of you. Dey's gwyne to be trouble, Mars Tom, " 'deed dey is" (219).

Huck bids the reader farewell: "So then we shoved for home, and not feeling very gay, neither" (219).

The boy who remained inside Mark Twain, hoping against hope to be free of all the Aunt Pollys in "sivilization," would have agreed wholeheartedly with one of Twain's more resounding lines: "In the first place God made idiots. This was for practice. Then He made School Boards."

I expect that Twain in the spirit of playfulness that is a vital part of *Tom Sawyer Abroad*, might have been beguiled by the use of that line of his by two high school students in Beaver Falls, Pennsylvania, not long ago. The students' adventure speaks to the continual contemporariness of Twain's view of the follies of official adults. And it also tells of the punishments in store for some young readers of Twain: not only being deprived of *Adventures of Huckleberry Finn* because of the word "nigger"—which is also in *Tom Sawyer Abroad*—but the kinds of sanctions inflicted on Jessica McCartney and Heidi Schanck, seniors at Blackhawk High School in Beaver Falls.

The two teenagers were considered sufficiently trustworthy to read school announcements over the public address system. To enliven the broadcasts, school officials gave them *A Teacher's Treasury of Quotations*. Looking through the anthology, the students found Twain's observation about idiots and school boards. It seemed to the young women that since there had been some recent controversy concerning the local school board, the quotation had a certain topical interest, and they read it over the public address system.

The principal was not amused. Charging the students with "disrespectful behavior," he punished them with a three-day in-school suspension. Futhermore, he commanded them to write letters of apology to each member of the school board, the teachers, and their fellow students. Until this crime, the perpetrators had had a clean record. God made school boards *and* principals.

Eventually, having been sharply criticized by the local newspaper, as well as some parents and a number of Mark Twain admirers, the principal reduced the suspension to two days and expunged the record of the students' transgression against common decency. Like Huck Finn, Jessica McCartney and Heidi Schanck would just as soon have escaped from civilization. And the author of *Tom Sawyer Abroad* would not have been at all surprised at the solemn stupidity of the principal.

Indeed, Mark Twain had experienced the solemn stupidity of censors himself, most egregiously with the bowdlerization of *Tom Sawyer Abroad* by Mary Mapes Dodge, who not only "purified" some of the language but even insisted that the illustrator put shoes on Huck — an act he might well have protested as violating his Eighth Amendment rights to be free of cruel and unusual punishment if Dodge had been an agent of the state. (For more dismaying details of her "high-minded" assault on Twain's manuscript of this novel, see the afterword by Thomas Inge.)

There is something about that other novel by Twain, *Adventures of Huckleberry Finn*, a story full of the surprises of growing up and out, that has encouraged feverish censorship since its publication. I've written about this phenomenon in schools — where it most often occurs — in a novel for young readers, *The Day They Came to Arrest the Book*.

Whatever the reasons that drive quite diverse people to want to exile Huck, the fundamental cause, it seems to me, is fear of his immediate honesty, which leads to his impatience with hypocrisy and pretense. And that leads to his irreverent independence of all pressures to conform. And many people, of all backgrounds, are deeply suspicious of incorrigible nonconformists.

In *Tom Sawyer Abroad*, there are passages of Huck's — and Jim's — spontaneous way of looking at the world, inside and out. And they, along with Tom, also see some of the savagery of existence, together with authentic decency. But as time went on, Twain grew more and more doubtful about the prospects for decency, and far less sanguine about our civilization's actually becoming civilized than was another original American. In an 1824 letter to Thomas Ludlow, Thomas Jefferson wrote:

I am eighty-one years of age, born where I now live, in the first range of mountains in the interior of our country. And I have observed this march of civilization advancing from the sea coast, passing over us like a cloud of light, increasing our knowledge and improving our condition, insomuch as that we are at this time more advanced in civilization here than the seaports were when I was a boy.

And where this progress will stop no one can say. Barbarism has, meantime, been receding before the steady step of amelioration and will in time, I trust, disappear from the earth.

Mark Twain, in "The Lowest Animal" (from the collection *Letters from the Earth*) had, to say the least, a decidedly different view.

I have been studying the traits and dispositions of the "lower animals" (so-called), and contrasting them with the traits and dispositions of man. I find the result humiliating to me. For it obliges me to renounce my allegiance to the Darwinian theory of the Ascent of Man from the Lower Animals; since it now seems plain to me that that theory ought to be vacated in favor of a new and truer one, this new and truer one to be named the *Descent* of Man from the Higher Animals.

Thankfully, Huck, Tom, and Jim deviated from this theory, in *Tom Sawyer Abroad* and their other appearance — and so did the author himself.

TOM SAWYER ABROAD

BY HUCK FINN

TOM SAWYER ABROAD,

BY MARK TWAIN

TOM SAWYER ABROAD

"WE CATCHED A LOT OF THE NICEST FISH YOU EVER SEE."

TOM SAWYER ABROAD

By HUCK FINN

EDITED BY

MARK TWAIN

With Illustrations by

DAN BEARD

NEW YORK
CHARLES L. WEBSTER & COMPANY
1894

PRESS OF
JENKINS & McCOWAN,
NEW YORK.

CONTENTS

6   CONTENTS.

ILLUSTRATIONS

TOM SAWYER ABROAD.

CHAPTER I.

TOM SEEKS NEW ADVENTURES.

Do you reckon Tom Sawyer was satisfied after all them adventures? I mean the adventures we had down the river, and the time we set the darky Jim free and Tom got shot in the leg. No, he was n't. It only just p'isoned him for more. That was all the effect it had. You see, when we three came back up the river in glory, as you may say, from that long travel, and the village received us with a torchlight procession and speeches, and everybody hurrah'd and shouted, it made us heroes, and that was what Tom Sawyer had always been hankering to be.

For a while he *was* satisfied. Everybody made much of him, and he tilted up his nose and stepped around the town as though he owned it. Some called him Tom Sawyer the Traveler, and that just swelled him up fit to bust. You see he laid over me and Jim considerable, because we only went down the river on a raft and came

back by the steamboat, but Tom went by the
steamboat both ways. The boys envied me and
Jim a good deal, but land! they just knuckled
to the dirt before TOM.

Well, I don't know ; maybe he might have
been satisfied if it had n't been for old Nat Parsons, which was postmaster, and powerful long
and slim, and kind o' good-hearted and silly, and
bald-headed, on account of his age, and about
the talkiest old cretur I ever see. For as much
as thirty years he 'd been the only man in the
village that had a reputation—I mean a reputation for being a traveler, and of course he was
mortal proud of it, and it was reckoned that in
the course of that thirty years he had told about
that journey over a million times and enjoyed it
every time. And now comes along a boy not
quite fifteen, and sets everybody admiring and
gawking over *his* travels, and it just give the poor
old man the high strikes. It made him sick to
listen to Tom, and to hear the people say "My
land!" "Did you ever!" "My goodness sakes
alive!" and all such things; but he could n't pull
away from it, any more than a fly that 's got its
hind leg fast in the molasses. And always when
Tom come to a rest, the poor old cretur would

chip in on *his* same old travels and work them
for all they were worth, but they were pretty
faded, and did n't go for much, and it was pitiful
to see.   And then Tom would take another in-
nings, and then the old man again — and so on,
and so on, for an hour and more, each trying to
beat out the other.

You see, Parsons' travels happened like this:
When he first got to be postmaster and was green
in the business, there come a letter for somebody
he did n't know, and there was n't any such person
in the village. Well, he did n't know what to do, nor
how to act, and there the letter stayed and stayed,
week in and week out, till the bare sight of it
give him a conniption.   The postage was n't paid
cı it, and that was another thing to worry about.
There was n't any way to collect that ten cents,
and he reckon'd the Gov'ment would hold him
responsible for it and maybe turn him out besides, when they found he had n't collected it.
Well, at last he could n't stand it any longer.   He
could n't sleep nights, he could n't eat, he was
thinned down to a shadder, yet he da'sn't ask
anybody's advice, for the very person he asked
for advice might go back on him and let the
Gov'ment know about the letter.   He had the

letter buried under the floor, but that did no good; if he happened to see a person standing over the place it 'd give him the cold shivers, and loaded him up with suspicions, and he would sit up that night till the town was as still and dark, and then he would sneak there and get it out and bury it in another place. Of course people got to avoiding him and shaking their heads and whispering, because, the way he was looking and acting, they judged he had killed somebody or done something terrible, they did n't know what, and if he had been a stranger they would 've lynched him.

Well, as I was saying, it got so he could n't stand it any longer; so he made up his mind to pull out for Washington, and just go to the President of the United States and make a clean breast of the whole thing, not keeping back an atom, and then fetch the letter out and lay it before the whole Gov'ment, and say, "Now, there she is — do with me what you 're a mind to; though as heaven is my judge I am an innocent man and not deserving cf the full penalties of the law and leaving behind me a family that must starve and yet had n't had a thing to do with it, which is the whole truth and I can swear to it."

So he did it. He had a little wee bit of steam-boating, and some stage-coaching, but all the rest of the way was horseback, and it took him three weeks to get to Washington. He saw lots of land and lots of villages and four cities. He was gone 'most eight weeks, and there never was such a proud man in the village as when he got back. His travels made him the greatest man in all that region, and the most talked about; and people come from as much as thirty miles back in the country, and from over in the Illinois bottoms, too, just to look at him — and there they 'd stand and gawk, and he 'd gabble. You never see any-thing like it.

Well, there was n't any way, now, to settle which was the greatest traveler; some said it was Nat, some said it was Tom. Everybody allowed that Nat had seen the most longitude, but they had to give in that whatever Tom was short in longitude he had made up in latitude and climate. It was about a stand-off; so both of them had to whoop up their dangerous adventures, and try to get ahead *that* way. That bullet-wound in Tom's leg was a tough thing for Nat Parsons to buck against, but he bucked the best he could; and at a disadvantage, too, for Tom did n't set still as

he 'd orter done, to be fair, but always got up
and sauntered around and worked his limp while
Nat was painting up the adventure that *he* had
in Washington; for Tom never let go that limp
when his leg got well, but practised it nights at
home, and kept it good as new right along.

Nat's adventure was like this; I don't know
how true it is; maybe he got it out of a paper, or
somewhere, but I will say this for him, that he
did know how to tell it. He could make anybody's flesh crawl, and he 'd turn pale and hold
his breath when he told it, and sometimes women
and girls got so faint they could n't stick it out.
Well, it was this way, as near as I can remember:

He come a-loping into Washington, and put up
his horse and shoved out to the President's house
with his letter, and they told him the President
was up to the Capitol, and just going to start for
Philadelphia—not a minute to lose if he wanted
to catch him. Nat 'most dropped, it made him so
sick. His horse was put up, and he did n't know
what *to* do. But just then along comes a darky
driving an old ramshackly hack, and he see his
chance. He rushes out and shouts: "A half a
dollar if you git me to the Capitol in half an hour,

and a quarter extra if you do it in twenty minutes ! "

" Done ! " says the darky.

Nat he jumped in and slammed the door, and
away they went a-ripping and a-tearing over the
roughest road a body ever see, and the racket of
it was something awful. Nat passed his arms
through the loops and hung on for life and death,
but pretty soon the hack hit a rock and flew up
in the air, and the bottom fell out, and when it
come down Nat's feet was on the ground, and he
see he was in the most desperate danger if he
could n't keep up with the hack. He was horrible
scared, but he laid into his work for all he was
worth, and hung tight to the arm-loops and made
his legs fairly fly. He yelled and shouted to the
driver to stop, and so did the crowds along the
street, for they could see his legs spinning along
under the coach, and his head and shoulders bob-
bing inside, through the windows, and he was in
awful danger ; but the more they all shouted the
more the nigger whooped and yelled and lashed
the horses and shouted, " Don't you fret, I 's gwine
to git you dah in time, boss ; I 's gwine to do it,
sho' ! " for you see he thought they were all hurrying him up, and of course he could n't hear

anything for the racket he was making. And so they went ripping along, and everybody just petrified to see it ; and when they got to the Capitol at last it was the quickest trip that ever was made, and everybody said so. The horses laid down, and Nat dropped, all tuckered out, and he was all dust and rags and barefooted ; but he was in time and just in time, and caught the President and give him the letter, and everything was all right, and the President give him a free pardon on the spot, and Nat give the nigger two extra quarters instead of one because he could see that if he had n't had the hack he would n't 'a' got there in time, nor anywhere near it.

It *was* a powerful good adventure, and Tom Sawyer had to work his bullet-wound mighty lively to hold his own against it.

Well, by and by Tom's glory got to paling down gradu'ly, on account of other things turning up for the people to talk about — first a horse-race, and on top of that a house afire, and on top of that the circus, and on top of that the eclipse ; and that started a revival, same as it always does, and by that time there was n't any more talk about Tom, so to speak, and you never see a person so sick and disgusted.

Pretty soon he got to worrying and fretting right along day in and day out, and when I asked him what *was* he in such a state about, he said it 'most broke his heart to think how time was slipping away, and him getting older and older, and no wars breaking out and no way of making a name for himself that he could see. Now that is the way boys is always thinking, but he was the first one I ever heard come out and say it.

So then he set to work to get up a plan to make him celebrated ; and pretty soon he struck it, and offered to take me and Jim in. Tom Sawyer was always free and generous that way. There's a plenty of boys that 's mighty good and friendly when *you* 've got a good thing, but when a good thing happens to come their way they don't say a word to you, and try to hog it all. That war n't ever Tom Sawyer's way, I can say that for him. There 's plenty of boys that will come hankering and groveling around you when you 've got an apple, and beg the core off of you ; but when they 've got one, and you beg for the core and remind them how you give them a core one time, they say thank you 'most to death, but there ain't a-going to be no core. But I notice they always git come up with; all you got to do is to wait.

Well, we went out in the woods on the hill, and Tom told us what it was. It was a crusade.

"What 's a crusade?" I says.

He looked scornful the way he 's always done when he was ashamed of a person, and says—

"Huck Finn, do you mean to tell me you don't know what a crusade is?"

"No," says I, "I don't. And I don't care to, nuther. I 've lived till now and done without it, and had my health, too. But as soon as you tell me, I 'll know, and that 's soon enough. I don't see any use in finding out things and clogging up my head with them when I may n't ever have any occasion to use 'em. There was Lance Williams, he learned how to talk Choctaw here till one come and dug his grave for him. Now, then, what 's a crusade? But I can tell you one thing before you begin; if it 's a patent-right, there 's no money in it. Bill Thompson he—"

"Patent-right!" says he. "I never see such an idiot. Why, a crusade is a kind of war."

I thought he must be losing his mind. But no, he was in real earnest, and went right on, perfectly ca'm:

"WE WENT OUT IN THE WOODS ON THE HILL, AND TOM TOLD US WHAT IT WAS.   IT WAS A CRUSADE."

"A crusade is a war to recover the Holy Land from the paynim."

"Which Holy Land?"

"Why, *the* Holy Land—there ain't but one."

"What do *we* want of it?"

"Why, can't you understand? It's in the hands of the paynim, and it's our duty to take it away from them."

"How did we come to let them git hold of it?"

"We did n't come to let them git hold of it. They always had it."

"Why, Tom, then it must belong to them, don't it?"

"Why of course it does. Who said it did n't?"

I studied over it, but could n't seem to git at the right of it, no way. I says:

"It's too many for me, Tom Sawyer. If I had a farm and it was mine, and another person wanted it, would it be right for him to—"

"Oh, shucks! you don't know enough to come in when it rains, Huck Finn. It ain't a farm, it's entirely different. You see, it's like this. They own the land, just the mere land, and that's all they *do* own; but it was our folks, our Jews and Christians, that made it holy, and so they have n't any business to be there defiling it. It's a shame, and we ought not to stand it a minute. We ought to march against them and take it away from them."

"Why, it does seem to me it 's the most mixed-up thing I ever see! Now if I had a farm and another person—"

"Don't I tell you it has n't got anything to do with farming? Farming is business, just common low-down business; that 's all it is, it 's all you can say for it ; but this is higher, this is religious, and totally different."

"Religious to go and take the land away from people that owns it?"

"Certainly ; it 's always been considered so."

Jim he shook his head, and says:

"Mars Tom, I reckon dey 's a mistake about it somers—dey mos' sholy is. I 's religious myself, en I knows plenty religious people, but I hain't run across none dat acts like dat."

It made Tom hot, and he says :

"Well, it 's enough to make a body sick, such mullet-headed ignorance! If either of you 'd read anything about history, you 'd know that Richard Cur de Loon, and the Pope, and Godfrey de Bulleyn, and lots more of the most noble-hearted and pious people in the world, hacked and ham-

mered at the paynims for more than two hundred
years trying to take their land away from them,
and swum neck-deep in blood the whole time—
and yet here 's a couple of sap-headed country
yahoos out in the backwoods of Missouri, setting
themselves up to know more about the rights
and wrongs of it than they did! Talk about
cheek!"

Well, of course, that put a more different light
on it, and me and Jim felt pretty cheap and ignorant, and wished we had n't been quite so
chipper. I could n't say nothing, and Jim he
could n't for a while; then he says:

"Well, den, I reckon it 's all right; beca'se ef
dey did n't know, dey ain't no use for po' ignorant folks like us to be trying to know; en so, ef
it 's our duty, we got to go en tackle it en do de
bes' we can. Same time, I feel as sorry for dem
paynims as Mars Tom. De hard part gwine to
be to kill folks dat a body hain't been 'quainted
wid and dat hain't done him no harm. Dat 's it,
you see. Ef we wuz to go 'mongst 'em, jist we
three, en say we 's hungry, en ast 'em for a bite
to eat, why, maybe dey's jist like yuther people.
Don't you reckon dey is? Why, *dey* 'd give it,
I know dey would, en den—"

"Then what?"

"Well, Mars Tom, my idea is like dis. It ain't no use, we *can't* kill dem po' strangers dat ain't doin' us no harm, till we 've had practice—I knows it perfectly well, Mars Tom—'deed I knows it perfectly well. But ef we takes a' ax or two, jist you en me en Huck, en slips acrost de river to-night arter de moon 's gone down, en kills dat sick fam'ly dat 's over on the Sny, en burns dey house down, en—"

"Oh, you make me tired!" says Tom. "I don't want to argue any more with people like you and Huck Finn, that 's always wandering from the subject, and ain't got any more sense than to try to reason out a thing that 's pure theology by the laws that protect real estate!"

Now that 's just where Tom Sawyer war n't fair. Jim did n't mean no harm, and I did n't mean no harm. We knowed well enough that he was right and we was wrong, and all we was after was to get at the *how* of it, and that was all; and the only reason he could n't explain it so we could understand it was because we was ignorant—yes, and pretty dull, too, I ain't deny-ing that; but, land! that ain't no crime, I should think.

But he would n't hear no more about it—just said if we had tackled the thing in the proper spirit, he would 'a' raised a couple of thousand knights and put them in steel armor from head to heel, and made me a lieutenant and Jim a sutler, and took the command himself and brushed the whole paynim outfit into the sea like flies and come back across the world in a glory like sunset. But he said we did n't know enough to take the chance when we had it, and he would n't ever offer it again. And he did n't. When he once got set, you could n't budge him.

But I did n't care much. I am peaceable, and don't get up rows with people that ain't doing nothing to me. I allowed if the paynim was satisfied I was, and we would let it stand at that.

Now Tom he got all that notion out of Walter Scott's book, which he was always reading. And it *was* a wild notion, because in my opinion he never could 've raised the men, and if he did, as like as not he would 've got licked. I took the books and read all about it, and as near as I could make it out, most of the folks that shook farming to go crusading had a mighty rocky time of it.

CHAPTER II.

WELL, Tom got up one thing after another, but they all had tender spots about 'em some-wheres, and he had to shove 'em aside. So at last he was about in despair. Then the St. Louis papers begun to talk a good deal about the bal-loon that was going to sail to Europe, and Tom sort of thought he wanted to go down and see what it looked like, but could n't make up his mind. But the papers went on talking, and so he allowed that maybe if he did n't go he might n't ever have another chance to see a bal-loon; and next, he found out that Nat Parsons was going down to see it, and that decided him, of course. He was n't going to have Nat Parsons coming back bragging about seeing the balloon, and him having to listen to it and keep quiet. So he wanted me and Jim to go too, and we went.

It was a noble big balloon, and had wings and fans and all sorts of things, and was n't like any

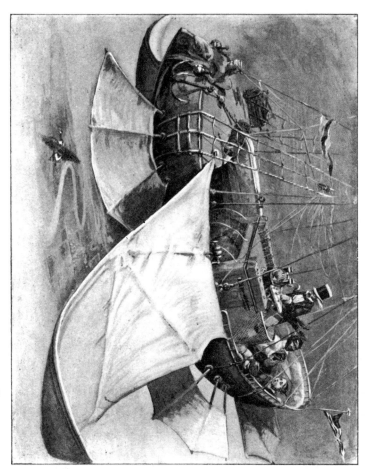

"HE SAID HE WOULD SAIL HIS BALLOON AROUND THE WORLD."

balloon you see in pictures. It was away out
toward the edge of town, in a vacant lot, corner
of Twelfth street; and there was a big crowd
around it, making fun of it, and making fun of
the man,—a lean pale feller with that soft kind
of moonlight in his eyes, you know,—and they
kept saying it would n't go. It made him hot to
hear them, and he would turn on them and
shake his fist and say they was animals and
blind, but some day they would find they had
stood face to face with one of the men that lifts
up nations and makes civilizations, and was too
dull to know it; and right here on this spot their
own children and grandchildren would build a
monument to him that would outlast a thousand
years, but his name would outlast the monument. And then the crowd would burst out in
a laugh again, and yell at him, and ask him what
was his name before he was married, and what
he would take to not do it, and what was his sister's cat's grandmother's name, and all the
things that a crowd says when they 've got hold
of a feller that they see they can plague. Well,
some things they said *was* funny,—yes, and
mighty witty too, I ain't denying that,—but all
the same it war n't fair nor brave, all them peo-

ple pitching on one, and they so glib and sharp,
and him without any gift of talk to answer back
with. But, good land! what did he want to
sass back for? You see, it could n't do him no
good, and it was just nuts for them. They *had*
him, you know. But that was his way. I
reckon he could n't help it; he was made so, I
judge. He was a good-enough sort of cretur, and
had n't no harm in him, and was just a genius,
as the papers said, which was n't his fault. We
can't all be sound: we 've got to be the way
we 're made. As near as I can make out, gen-
iuses think they know it all, and so they won't
take people's advice, but always go their own
way, which makes everybody forsake them and
despise them, and that is perfectly natural. If
they was humbler, and listened and tried to
learn, it would be better for them.

The part the professor was in was like a boat,
and was big and roomy, and had water-tight
lockers around the inside to keep all sorts of
things in, and a body could sit on them, and
make beds on them, too. We went aboard, and
there was twenty people there, snooping around
and examining, and old Nat Parsons was there,
too. The professor kept fussing around, getting

ready, and the people went ashore, drifting out one at a time, and old Nat he was the last. Of course it would n't do to let him go out behind *us*. We must n't budge till he was gone, so we could be last ourselves.

But he was gone now, so it was time for us to follow. I heard a big shout, and turned around —the city was dropping from under us like a shot! It made me sick all through, I was so scared. Jim turned gray and could n't say a word, and Tom did n't say nothing, but looked excited. The city went on dropping down, and down, and down; but we did n't seem to be doing nothing but just hang in the air and stand still. The houses got smaller and smaller, and the city pulled itself together, closer and closer, and the men and wagons got to looking like ants and bugs crawling around, and the streets like threads and cracks; and then it all kind of melted together, and there was n't any city any more: it was only a big scar on the earth, and it seemed to me a body could see up the river and down the river about a thousand miles, though of course it was n't so much. By and by the earth was a ball—just a round ball, of a dull color, with shiny stripes wriggling and winding

around over it, which was rivers. The Widder
Douglas always told me the earth was round
like a ball, but I never took any stock in a lot of
them superstitions o' hers, and of course I paid
no attention to that one, because I could see myself that the world was the shape of a plate, and
flat. I used to go up on the hill, and take a look
around and prove it for myself, because I reckon
the best way to get a sure thing on a fact is to
go and examine for yourself, and not take anybody's say-so. But I had to give in, now, that
the widder was right. That is, she was right as
to the rest of the world, but she war n't right
about the part our village is in ; that part is the
shape of a plate, and flat, I take my oath !

The professor had been quiet all this time, as
if he was asleep ; but he broke loose now, and
he was mighty bitter. He says something like
this :

"Idiots ! They said it would n't go ; and they
wanted to examine it, and spy around and get
the secret of it out of me. But I beat them.
Nobody knows the secret but me. Nobody
knows what makes it move but me; and it 's a
new power—a new power, and a thousand times
the strongest in the earth ! Steam 's foolishness

to it! They said I could n't go to Europe. To Europe! Why, there's power aboard to last five years, and feed for three months. They are fools! What do they know about it? Yes, and they said my air-ship was flimsy. Why, she's good for fifty years! I can sail the skies all my life if I want to, and steer where I please, though they laughed at that, and said I could n't. Could n't steer! Come here, boy; we'll see. You press these buttons as I tell you."

He made Tom steer the ship all about and every which way, and learnt him the whole thing in nearly no time; and Tom said it was perfectly easy. He made him fetch the ship down 'most to the earth, and had him spin her along so close to the Illinois prairies that a body could talk to the farmers, and hear everything they said perfectly plain; and he flung out printed bills to them that told about the balloon, and said it was going to Europe. Tom got so he could steer straight for a tree till he got nearly to it, and then dart up and skin right along over the top of it. Yes, and he showed Tom how to land her; and he done it first-rate, too, and set her down in the prairies as soft as wool. But the minute we started to skip out the professor says, " No, you

don't ! " and shot her up in the air again. It was
awful. I begun to beg, and so did Jim; but it
only give his temper a rise, and he begun to rage
around and look wild out of his eyes, and I was
scared of him.

Well, then he got on to his troubles again,
and mourned and grumbled about the way he
was treated, and could n't seem to git over it,
and especially people's saying his ship was flimsy.
He scoffed at that, and at their saying she war n't
simple and would be always getting out of order.
Get out of order ! That graveled him; he said
that she could n't any more get out of order than
the solar sister.

He got worse and worse, and I never see a person take on so. It give me the cold shivers to
see him, and so it did Jim. By and by he got to
yelling and screaming, and then he swore the
world should n't ever have his secret at all now,
it had treated him so mean. He said he would
sail his balloon around the globe just to show
what he could do, and then he would sink it in
the sea, and sink us all along with it, too. Well,
it was the awfullest fix to be in, and here was
night coming on !

He give us something to eat, and made us go

" AND HERE WAS NIGHT COMING ON!"

to the other end of the boat, and he laid down on a locker, where he could boss all the works, and put his old pepper-box revolver under his head, and said if anybody come fooling around there trying to land her, he would kill him.

We set scrunched up together, and thought considerable, but did n't say much—only just a word once in a while when a body had to say something or bust, we was *so* scared and worried. The night dragged along slow and lonesome. We was pretty low down, and the moonshine made everything soft and pretty, and the farmhouses looked snug and homeful, and we could hear the farm sounds, and wished we could be down there; but, laws! we just slipped along over them like a ghost, and never left a track.

Away in the night, when all the sounds was late sounds, and the air had a late feel, and a late smell, too,—about a two-o'clock feel, as near as I could make out,—Tom said the professor was so quiet this time he must be asleep, and we 'd better—

"Better what?" I says in a whisper, and feeling sick all over, because I knowed what he was thinking about.

"Better slip back there and tie him, and land the ship," he says.

I says: "No, sir! Don't you budge, Tom Sawyer."

And Jim—well, Jim was kind o' gasping, he was so scared. He says:

"Oh, Mars Tom, *don't!* Ef you teches him, we 's gone—we 's gone sho'! I ain't gwine anear him, not for nothin' in dis worl'. Mars Tom, he 's plumb crazy."

Tom whispers and says: "That 's *why* we 've got to do something. If he was n't crazy I would n't give shucks to be anywhere but here; you could n't hire me to get out,—now that I 've got used to this balloon and over the scare of being cut loose from the solid ground,—if he was in his right mind. But it 's no good politics, sailing around like this with a person that 's out of his head, and says he 's going round the world and then drown us all. We 've *got* to do something, I tell you, and do it before he wakes up, too, or we may n't ever get another chance. Come!"

But it made us turn cold and creepy just to think of it, and we said we would n't budge. So Tom was for slipping back there by himself to see if he could n't get at the steering-gear and land the ship. We begged and begged him not to, but it war n't no use; so he got down on his hands and knees, and begun to crawl an inch at a time, we a-holding our breath and watching. After he got to the middle of the boat he crept slower than ever, and it did seem like years to me. But at last we see him get to the professor's head, and sort of raise up soft and look a good spell in his face and listen. Then we see him begin to inch along again toward the professor's feet where the steering-buttons was. Well, he got there all safe, and was reaching slow and steady toward the buttons, but he knocked down something that made a noise, and we see him slump down flat an' soft in the bottom, and lay still. The professor stirred, and says, "What 's that?" But everybody kept dead still and quiet, and he begun to mutter and mumble and nestle, like a person that's going to wake up, and I thought I was going to die, I was so worried and scared.

Then a cloud slid over the moon, and I 'most cried, I was so glad. She buried herself deeper and deeper into the cloud, and it got so dark we could n't see Tom. Then it began to sprinkle rain, and we could hear the professor fussing at his

ropes and things and abusing the weather. We
was afraid every minute he would touch Tom,
and then we would be goners, and no help; but
Tom was already on his way back, and when we
felt his hands on our knees my breath stopped
sudden, and my heart fell down 'mongst my
other works, because I could n't tell in the dark
but it might be the professor, which I thought
it *was*.

Dear! I was so glad to have him back that I
was just as near happy as a person could be that
was up in the air that way with a deranged man.
You can't land a balloon in the dark, and so I
hoped it would keep on raining, for I did n't
want Tom to go meddling any more and make
us so awful uncomfortable. Well, I got my
wish. It drizzled and drizzled along the rest of
the night, which was n't long, though it did seem
so; and at daybreak it cleared, and the world
looked mighty soft and gray and pretty, and the
forests and fields so good to see again, and the
horses and cattle standing sober and thinking.
Next, the sun come a-blazing up gay and splendid, and then we began to feel rusty and stretchy,
and first we knowed we was all asleep.

CHAPTER III.

TOM EXPLAINS.

WE went to sleep about four o'clock, and woke up about eight. The professor was setting back there at his end, looking glum. He pitched us some breakfast, but he told us not to come abaft the midship compass. That was about the middle of the boat. Well, when you are sharp-set, and you eat and satisfy yourself, everything looks pretty different from what it done before. It makes a body feel pretty near comfortable, even when he is up in a balloon with a genius. We got to talking together.

There was one thing that kept bothering me, and by and by I says:

"Tom, did n't we start east?"

"Yes."

"How fast have we been going?"

"Well, you heard what the professor said when he was raging round. Sometimes, he said, we was making fifty miles an hour, sometimes ninety, sometimes a hundred; said that with a gale to help he could make three hundred any time, and

said if he wanted the gale, and wanted it blowing the right direction, he only had to go up
higher or down lower to find it."

"Well, then, it 's just as I reckoned. The professor lied."

"Why ?"

"Because if we was going so fast we ought to
be past Illinois, ought n't we ?"

"Certainly."

"Well, we ain't."

"What 's the reason we ain't ?"

"I know by the color. We 're right over Illinois yet. And you can see for yourself that
Indiana ain't in sight."

"I wonder what 's the matter with you, Huck.
You know by the *color ?*"

"Yes, of course I do."

"What 's the color got to do with it ?"

"It 's got everything to do with it. Illinois is
green, Indiana is pink. You show me any pink
down here, if you can. No, sir ; it 's green."

"Indiana *pink ?* Why, what a lie ?"

"It ain't no lie ; I 've seen it on the map, and
it 's pink."

You never see a person so aggravated and disgusted. He says :

"Well, if I was such a numskull as you, Huck Finn, I would jump over. Seen it on the map! Huck Finn, did you reckon the States was the same color out of doors as they are on the map?"

"Tom Sawyer, what's a map for? Ain't it to learn you facts?"

"Of course."

"Well, then, how's it going to do that if it tells lies? That's what I want to know."

"Shucks, you muggins! It don't tell lies."

"It don't, don't it?"

"No, it don't."

"All right, then; if it don't, there ain't no two States the same color. You git around *that*, if you can, Tom Sawyer."

He see I had him, and Jim see it too; and I tell you, I felt pretty good, for Tom Sawyer was always a hard person to git ahead of. Jim slapped his leg and says:

"I tell *you!* dat's smart, dat's right down smart. Ain't no use, Mars Tom; he got you *dis* time, sho!" He slapped his leg again, and says, "My *lan'*, but it was smart one!"

I never felt so good in my life; and yet *I* did n't know I was saying anything much till it was out. I was just mooning along, perfectly careless, and not expecting anything was going to happen, and never *thinking* of such a thing at all, when, all of a sudden, out it come. Why, it was just as much a surprise to me as it was to any of them. It was just the same way it is when a person is munching along on a hunk of corn-pone, and not thinking about anything, and all of a sudden bites into a di'mond. Now all that *he* knows first off is that it 's some kind of gravel he 's bit into ; but he don't find out it 's a di'mond till he gits it out and brushes off the sand and crumbs and one thing or another, and has a look at it, and then he 's surprised and glad—yes, and proud too ; though when you come to look the thing straight in the eye, he ain't entitled to as much credit as he would 'a' been if he 'd been *hunting* di'monds. You can see the difference easy if you think it over. You see, an accident, that way, ain't fairly as big a thing as a thing that 's done a-purpose. Anybody could find that di'mond in that corn-pone ; but mind you, it 's got to be somebody that 's got *that kind of a corn-pone.* That 's where that feller's credit comes in, you see ; and that 's where mine comes in. I don't claim no great things,—I don't reckon I could 'a' done it again,—but I done it that time ;

that 's all I claim.   And I had n't no more idea I
could do such a thing, and war n't any more
thinking about it or trying to, than you be this
minute.   Why, I was just as cam, a body could n't
be any cammer, and yet, all of a sudden, out it
come.   I 've often thought of that time, and I
can remember just the way everything looked,
same as if it was only last week.   I can see it all :
beautiful rolling country with woods and fields
and lakes for hundreds and hundreds of miles all
around, and towns and villages scattered everywheres under us, here and there and yonder ; and
the professor mooning over a chart on his little
table, and Tom's cap flopping in the rigging
where it was hung up to dry.   And one thing in
particular was a bird right alongside, not ten foot
off, going our way and trying to keep up, but
losing ground all the time ; and a railroad train
doing the same thing down there, sliding among
the trees and farms, and pouring out a long cloud
of black smoke and now and then a little puff of
white ; and when the white was gone so long
you had almost forgot it, you would hear a little
faint toot, and that was the whistle.   And we
left the bird and the train both behind, '*way* behind, and done it easy too.

But Tom he was huffy, and said me and Jim
was a couple of ignorant blatherskites, and then
he says :

" Suppose there 's a brown calf and a big brown
dog, and an artist is making a picture of them.
What is the *main* thing that that artist has got to
do ? He has got to paint them so you can tell
them apart the minute you look at them, hain't
he ? Of course. Well, then, do you want him
to go and paint *both* of them brown ? Certainly
you don't. He paints one of them blue, and then
you can't make no mistake. It 's just the same
with the maps. That 's why they make every
State a different color ; it ain't to deceive you,
it 's to keep you from deceiving yourself."

But I could n't see no argument about that, and
neither could Jim. Jim shook his head, and says :

" Why, Mars Tom, if you knowed what chuckle-
heads dem painters is, you 'd wait a long time
before you 'd fetch one er *dem* in to back up a
fac'. I 's gwine to tell you, den you kin see for
youself. I see one of 'em a-paintin' away, one
day, down in ole Hank Wilson's back lot, en I
went down to see, en he was paintin' dat old
brindle cow wid de near horn gone—you knows
de one I means. En I ast him what he 's paintin'

her for, en he say when he git her painted, de picture 's wuth a hundred dollars. Mars Tom, he could a got de cow fer fifteen, en I *tole* him so. Well, sah, if you 'll b'lieve me, he jes' shuck his head, dat painter did, en went on a-dobbin'. Bless you, Mars Tom, *dey* don't know nothin'."

Tom he lost his temper. I notice a person 'most always does that 's got laid out in an argument. He told us to shut up, and maybe we 'd feel better. Then he see a town clock away off down yonder, and he took up the glass and looked at it, and then looked at his silver turnip, and then at the clock, and then at the turnip again, and says:

"That 's funny! That clock 's near about an hour fast."

So he put up his turnip. Then he see another clock, and took a look, and it was an hour fast too. That puzzled him.

"That 's a mighty curious thing," he says. " I don't understand it."

Then he took the glass and hunted up another clock, and sure enough it was an hour fast too. Then his eyes began to spread and his breath to come out kinder gaspy like, and he says:

"Ger-reat Scott, it 's the *longitude!*"

I says, considerably scared :

" Well, what 's been and gone and happened now ? "

"Why, the thing that 's happened is that this old bladder has slid over Illinois and Indiana and Ohio like nothing, and this is the east end of Pennsylvania or New York, or somewheres around there."

" Tom Sawyer, you don't mean it ! "

" Yes, I do, and it 's dead sure. We 've covered about fifteen degrees of longitude since we left St. Louis yesterday afternoon, and them clocks are *right*. We 've come close on to eight hundred miles."

I did n't believe it, but it made the cold streaks trickle down my back just the same. In my experience I knowed it would n't take much short of two weeks to do it down the Mississippi on a raft.

Jim was working his mind and studying. Pretty soon he says :

" Mars Tom, did you say dem clocks uz right ? "

" Yes, they 're right."

" Ain't yo' watch right, too ? "

" She 's right for St. Louis, but she 's an hour wrong for here."

"YOU WANT TO LEAVE ME. DON'T TRY TO DENY IT."

"Mars Tom, is you tryin' to let on dat de time ain't de *same* everywheres?"

"No, it ain't the same everywheres, by a long shot."

Jim looked distressed, and says:

"It grieves me to hear you talk like dat, Mars Tom; I's right down ashamed to hear you talk like dat, arter de way you's been raised. Yassir, it'd break yo' Aunt Polly's heart to hear you."

Tom was astonished. He looked Jim over, wondering, and did n't say nothing, and Jim went on:

"Mars Tom, who put de people out yonder in St. Louis? De Lord done it. Who put de people here whar we is? De Lord done it. Ain' dey bofe his children? 'Cose dey is. *Well*, den! is he gwine to *scriminate* 'twixt 'em?"

"Scriminate! I never heard such ignorance. There ain't no discriminating about it. When he makes you and some more of his children black, and makes the rest of us white, what du you call that?"

Jim see the p'int. He was stuck. He could n't answer. Tom says:

"He does discriminate, you see, when he wants to; but this case *here* ain't no discrimination of his, it 's man's. The Lord made the day, and he made the night ; but he did n't invent the hours, and he didn't distribute them around. Man did that."

" Mars Tom, is dat so ? Man done it ? "

" Certainly."

" Who tole him he could ? "

" Nobody. He never asked."

Jim studied a minute, and says :

" Well, dat do beat me. I would n't 'a' tuck no sich resk. But some people ain't scared o' nothin'. Dey bangs right ahead ; *dey* don't care what happens. So den dey 's allays an hour's diff'unce everywhah, Mars Tom ? "

" An hour ? No ! It 's four minutes difference for every degree of longitude, you know. Fifteen of 'em 's an hour, thirty of 'em 's two hours, and so on. When it 's one o'clock Tuesday morning in England, it 's eight o'clock the night before in New York."

Jim moved a little way along the locker, and you could see he was insulted. He kept shaking his head and muttering, and so I slid along to him and patted him on the leg, and petted him up, and got him over the worst of his feelings, and then he says :

"Mars Tom talkin' sich talk as dat! Choosday in one place en Monday in t' other, bofe in the same day! Huck, dis ain't no place to joke — up here whah we is. Two days in one day! How you gwine to got two days inter one day? Can't git two hours inter one hour, kin you? Can't git two niggers inter one nigger skin, kin you? Can't git two gallons of whisky inter a one-gallon jug, kin you? No, sir, 't would strain de jug. Yes, en even den you could n't, *I* don't believe. Why, looky here, Huck, s'posen de Choosday was New Year's — now den! is you gwine to tell me it 's dis year in one place en las' year in t' other, bofe in de identical same minute? It 's de beatenest rubbage! I can't stan' it — I can't stan' to hear tell 'bout it." Then he begun to shiver and turn gray, and Tom says:

"*Now* what 's the matter? What 's the trouble?"

Jim could hardly speak, but he says:

"Mars Tom, you ain't jokin', en it 's *so?*"

"No I'm not, and it *is* so."

Jim shivered again, and says:

"Den dat Monday could be de las' day, en dey would n't be no las' day in England, en de dead would n't be called. We must n't go over dah,

Mars Tom. Please git him to turn back; I wants to be whah —"

All of a sudden we see something, and all jumped up, and forgot everything and begun to gaze. Tom says:

"Ain't that the —" He catched his breath, then says: "It *is*, sure as you live! It's the ocean!"

That made me and Jim catch our breath, too. Then we all stood petrified but happy, for none of us had ever seen an ocean, or ever expected to. Tom kept muttering:

"Atlantic Ocean — Atlantic. Land, don't it sound great! And that's *it* — and *we* are looking at it — we! Why, it's just too splendid to believe!"

Then we see a big bank of black smoke; and when we got nearer, it was a city — and a monster she was, too, with a thick fringe of ships around one edge; and we wondered if it was New York, and begun to jaw and dispute about it, and, first we knowed, it slid from under us and went flying behind, and here we was, out over the very ocean itself, and going like a cyclone. Then we woke up, I tell you!

We made a break aft and raised a wail, and begun to beg the professor to turn back and land us, but he jerked out his pistol and motioned us back, and we went, but nobody will ever know how bad we felt.

The land was gone, all but a little streak, like a snake, away off on the edge of the water, and down under us was just ocean, ocean, ocean — millions of miles of it, heaving and pitching and squirming, and white sprays blowing from the wave-tops, and only a few ships in sight, wallowing around and laying over, first on one side and then on t' other, and sticking their bows under and then their sterns; and before long there war n't no ships at all, and we had the sky and the whole ocean all to ourselves, and the roomiest place I ever see and the lonesomest.

CHAPTER IV.

STORM.

AND it got lonesomer and lonesomer. There was the big sky up there, empty and awful deep; and the ocean down there without a thing on it but just the waves. All around us was a ring, where the sky and the water come together; yes, a monstrous big ring it was, and we right in the dead center of it—plumb in the center. We was racing along like a prairie fire, but it never made any difference, we could n't seem to git past that center no way. I could n't see that we ever gained an inch on that ring. It made a body feel creepy, it was so curious and unaccountable.

Well, everything was so awful still that we got to talking in a very low voice, and kept on getting creepier and lonesomer and less and less talky, till at last the talk ran dry altogether, and we just set there and "thunk," as Jim calls it, and never said a word the longest time.

The professor never stirred till the sun was overhead, then he stood up and put a kind of

"THE PROFESSOR SAID HE WOULD KEEP UP THIS HUNDRED-MILE
GAIT TILL TO-MORROW."

triangle to his eye, and Tom said it was a sextant and he was taking the sun to see whereabouts the balloon was. Then he ciphered a little and looked in a book, and then he begun to carry on again. He said lots of wild things, and amongst others he said he would keep up this hundred-mile gait till the middle of to-morrow afternoon, and then he'd land in London.

We said we would be humbly thankful.

He was turning away, but he whirled around when we said that, and give us a long look of his blackest kind — one of the maliciousest and sus-piciousest looks I ever see. Then he says :

" You want to leave me. Don't try to deny it."

We did n't know what to say, so we held in and didn't say nothing at all.

He went aft and set down, but he could n't seem to git that thing out of his mind. Every now and then he would rip out something about it, and try to make us answer him, but we das n't.

It got lonesomer and lonesomer right along, and it did seem to me I could n't stand it. It was still worse when night begun to come on. By and by Tom pinched me and whispers :

" Look ! "

I took a glance aft, and see the professor taking a whet out of a bottle. I did n't like the looks of that. By and by he took another drink, and pretty soon he begun to sing. It was dark now, and getting black and stormy. He went on singing, wilder and wilder, and the thunder begun to mutter, and the wind to wheeze and moan amongst the ropes, and altogether it was awful. It got so black we could n't see him any more, and wished we could n't hear him, but we could. Then he got still; but he war n't still ten minutes till we got suspicious, and wished he would start up his noise again, so we could tell where he was. By and by there was a flash of lightning, and we see him start to get up, but he staggered and fell down. We heard him scream out in the dark :

"They don't want to go to England. All right, I 'll change the course. They want to leave me. I know they do. Well, they shall— and *now!*"

I 'most died when he said that. Then he was still again,—still so long I could n't bear it, and it did seem to me the lightning would n't *ever* come again. But at last there was a blessed flash, and there he was, on his hands and knees, crawling, and not four feet from us. My, but

"THE THUNDER BOOMED, AND THE LIGHTNING GLARED, AND THE
WIND SCREAMED IN THE RIGGING."

his eyes was terrible! He made a lunge for
Tom, and says, "Overboard *you* go!" but it
was already pitch-dark again, and I could n't
see whether he got him or not, and Tom did n't
make a sound.

There was another long, horrible wait; then
there was a flash, and I see Tom's head sink
down outside the boat and disappear. He was
on the rope-ladder that dangled down in the air
from the gunnel. The professor let off a shout
and jumped for him, and straight off it was
pitch-dark again, and Jim groaned out, "Po'
Mars Tom, he 's a goner!" and made a jump
for the professor, but the professor war n't there.

Then we heard a couple of terrible screams,
and then another not so loud, and then another
that was 'way below, and you could only *just*
hear it; and I heard Jim say, "Po' Mars Tom!"

Then it was awful still, and I reckon a person
could 'a' counted four thousand before the next
flash come. When it come I see Jim on his
knees, with his arms on the locker and his face
buried in them, and he was crying. Before I
could look over the edge it was all dark again,
and I was glad, because I did n't want to see.
But when the next flash come, I was watching,

and down there I see somebody a-swinging in the wind on the ladder, and it was Tom!

"Come up!" I shouts; "come up, Tom!"

His voice was so weak, and the wind roared so, I could n't make out what he said, but I thought he asked was the professor up there. I shouts:

"No, he 's down in the ocean! Come up! Can we help you?"

Of course, all this in the dark.

"Huck, who is you hollerin' at?"

"I 'm hollerin' at Tom."

"Oh, Huck, how kin you act so, when you know po' Mars Tom 's—" Then he let off an awful scream, and flung his head and his arms back and let off another one, because there was a white glare just then, and he had raised up his face just in time to see Tom's, as white as snow, rise above the gunnel and look him right in the eye. He thought it was Tom's ghost, you see.

Tom clumb aboard, and when Jim found it *was* him, and not his ghost, he hugged him, and called him all sorts of loving names, and carried on like he was gone crazy, he was so glad. Says I:

"What did you wait for, Tom? Why did n't you come up at first?"

" I das n't, Huck. I knowed somebody plunged down past me, but I did n't know who it was in the dark. It could 'a' been you, it could 'a' been Jim."

That was the way with Tom Sawyer—always sound. He war n't coming up till he knowed where the professor was.

The storm let go about this time with all its might ; and it was dreadful the way the thunder boomed and tore, and the lightning glared out, and the wind sung and screamed in the rigging, and the rain come down. One second you could n't see your hand before you, and the next you could count the threads in your coat-sleeve, and see a whole wide desert of waves pitching and tossing through a kind of veil of rain. A storm like that is the loveliest thing there is, but it ain't at its best when you are up in the sky and lost, and it 's wet and lonesome, and there 's just been a death in the family.

We set there huddled up in the bow, and talked low about the poor professor ; and everybody was sorry for him, and sorry the world had made fun of him and treated him so harsh, when he was doing the best he could, and had n't a friend nor nobody to encourage him and keep him from brooding his mind away and going deranged. There was plenty of clothes and blankets and everything at the other end, but we thought we 'd ruther take the rain than go meddling back there.

CHAPTER V.

LAND.

WE tried to make some plans, but we could n't come to no agreement. Me and Jim was for turning around and going back home, but Tom allowed that by the time daylight come, so we could see our way, we would be so far toward England that we might as well go there, and come back in a ship, and have the glory of saying we done it.

About midnight the storm quit and the moon come out and lit up the ocean, and we begun to feel comfortable and drowsy; so we stretched out on the lockers and went to sleep, and never woke up again till sun-up. The sea was sparkling like di'monds, and it was nice weather, and pretty soon our things was all dry again.

We went aft to find some breakfast, and the first thing we noticed was that there was a dim light burning in a compass back there under a hood. Then Tom was disturbed. He says:

" You know what that means, easy enough.

It means that somebody has got to stay on watch and steer this thing the same as he would a ship, or she 'll wander around and go wherever the wind wants her to."

"Well," I says, "what 's she been doing since —er—since we had the accident?"

"Wandering," he says, kinder troubled — "wandering, without any doubt. She 's in a wind, now, that 's blowing her south of east. We don't know how long that 's been going on, either."

So then he p'inted her east, and said he would hold her there till we rousted out the breakfast. The professor had laid in everything a body could want; he could n't 'a' been better fixed. There was n't no milk for the coffee, but there was water, and everything else you could want, and a charcoal stove and the fixings for it, and pipes and cigars and matches; and wine and liquor, which war n't in our line; and books, and maps, and charts, and an accordion; and furs, and blankets, and no end of rubbish, like brass beads and brass jewelry, which Tom said was a sure sign that he had an idea of visiting among savages. There was money, too. Yes, the professor was well enough fixed.

"' RUN! RUN FO' YO' LIFE!'"

After breakfast Tom learned me and Jim how to steer, and divided us all up into four-hour watches, turn and turn about; and when his watch was out I took his place, and he got out the professor's papers and pens and wrote a letter home to his Aunt Polly, telling her everything that had happened to us, and dated it "*In the Welkin, approaching England*," and folded it together and stuck it fast with a red wafer, and directed it, and wrote above the direction, in big writing, "*From Tom Sawyer, the Erronort*," and said it would stump old Nat Parsons, the postmaster, when it come along in the mail. I says:

"Tom Sawyer, this ain't no welkin; it 's a balloon."

"Well, now, who *said* it was a welkin, smarty?"

"You 've wrote it on the letter, anyway."

"What of it? That don't mean that the balloon 's the welkin."

"Oh, I thought it did. Well, then, what is a welkin?"

I see in a minute he was stuck. He raked and scraped around in his mind, but he could n't find nothing, so he had to say:

"*I* don't know, and nobody don't know. It 's just a word, and it 's a mighty good word, too. There ain't many that lays over it. I don't believe there 's *any* that does."

"Shucks!" I says. "But what does it *mean?* —that 's the p'int."

"*I* don't know what it means, I tell you. It 's a word that people uses for — for — well, it 's ornamental. They don't put ruffles on a shirt to keep a person warm, do they?"

"Course they don't."

"But they put them *on*, don't they?"

"Yes."

"All right, then; that letter I wrote is a shirt, and the welkin 's the ruffle on it."

I judged that that would gravel Jim, and it did.

"Now, Mars Tom, it ain't no use to talk like dat; en, moreover, it 's sinful. You knows a letter ain't no shirt, en dey ain't no ruffles on it, nuther. Dey ain't no place to put 'em on; you can't put 'em on, and dey would n't stay ef you did."

"Oh, *do* shut up, and wait till something 's started that you know something about."

"Why, Mars Tom, sholy you can't mean to say I don't know about shirts, when, goodness knows, I 's toted home de washin' ever sence—"

"I tell you, this has n't got anything to *do* with shirts.   I only—"

"Why, Mars Tom, you said yo'self dat a letter—"

"Do you want to drive me crazy ?   Keep still. I only used it as a metaphor."

That word kinder bricked us up for a minute. Then Jim says — rather timid, because he see Tom was getting pretty tetchy :

"Mars Tom, what is a metaphor ?"

"A metaphor 's a—well, it 's a—a—a metaphor 's an illustration."   He see *that* did n't git home, so he tried again.   "When I say birds of a feather flocks together, it 's a metaphorical way of saying—"

"But dey *don't*, Mars Tom.   No, sir, 'deed dey don't.   Dey ain't no feathers dat 's more alike den a bluebird en a jaybird, but ef you waits till you catches *dem* birds together, you 'll—"

"Oh, give us a rest !   You can't get the simplest little thing through your thick skull.   Now don't bother me any more."

Jim was satisfied to stop.   He was dreadful pleased with himself for catching Tom out.

The minute Tom begun to talk about birds I
judged he was a goner, because Jim knowed
more about birds than both of us put together.
You see, he had killed hundreds and hundreds
of them, and that 's the way to find out about
birds. That 's the way people does that writes
books about birds, and loves them so that
they 'll go hungry and tired and take any
amount of trouble to find a new bird and kill
it. Their name is ornithologers, and I could
have been an ornithologer myself, because I
always loved birds and creatures; and I started
out to learn how to be one, and I see a bird
setting on a limb of a high tree, singing with its
head tilted back and its mouth open, and before
I thought I fired, and his song stopped and he
fell straight down from the limb, all limp like a
rag, and I run and picked him up and he was
dead, and his body was warm in my hand, and
his head rolled about this way and that, like his
neck was broke, and there was a little white
skin over his eyes, and one little drop of blood
on the side of his head; and, laws! I could n't
see nothing more for the tears; and I hain't
never murdered no creature since that war n't
doing me no harm, and I ain't going to.

But I was aggravated about that welkin. I wanted to know. I got the subject up again, and then Tom explained, the best he could. He said when a person made a big speech the newspapers said the shouts of the people made the welkin ring. He said they always said that, but none of them ever told what it was, so he allowed it just meant outdoors and up high. Well, that seemed sensible enough, so I was satisfied, and said so. That pleased Tom and put him in a good humor again, and he says:

"Well, it 's all right, then; and we 'll let bygones be bygones. I don't know for certain what a welkin is, but when we land in London we 'll make it ring, anyway, and don't you forget it."

He said an erronort was a person who sailed around in balloons; and said it was a mighty sight finer to be Tom Sawyer the Erronort than to be Tom Sawyer the Traveler, and we would be heard of all round the world, if we pulled through all right, and so he would n't give shucks to be a traveler now.

Toward the middle of the afternoon we got everything ready to land, and we felt pretty good, too, and proud; and we kept watching with the glasses, like Columbus discovering America. But we could n't see nothing but ocean. The afternoon wasted out and the sun shut down, and still there war n't no land any-wheres. We wondered what was the matter, but reckoned it would come out all right, so we went on steering east, but went up on a higher level so we would n't hit any steeples or moun-tains in the dark.

It was my watch till midnight, and then it was Jim's; but Tom stayed up, because he said ship-captains done that when they was making the land, and did n't stand no regular watch.

Well, when daylight come, Jim give a shout, and we jumped up and looked over, and there was the land sure enough,—land all around, as far as you could see, and perfectly level and yal-ler. We did n't know how long we 'd been over it. There war n't no trees, nor hills, nor rocks, nor towns, and Tom and Jim had took it for the sea. They took it for the sea in a dead cam; but we was so high up, anyway, that if it had been the sea and rough, it would 'a' looked smooth, all the same, in the night, that way.

We was all in a powerful excitement now, and grabbed the glasses and hunted everywheres for

"AND THERE WAS THE LION, A-RIPPING AROUND UNDER ME."

London, but could n't find hair nor hide of it, nor any other settlement,—nor any sign of a lake or a river, either. Tom was clean beat. He said it war n't his notion of England; he thought England looked like America, and always had that idea. So he said we better have breakfast, and then drop down and inquire the quickest way to London. We cut the breakfast pretty short, we was so impatient. As we slanted along down, the weather began to moderate, and pretty soon we shed our furs. But it kept *on* moderating, and in a precious little while it was 'most too moderate. We was close down, now, and just blistering!

We settled down to within thirty foot of the land,—that is, it was land if sand is land; for this was n't anything but pure sand. Tom and me clumb down the ladder and took a run to stretch our legs, and it felt amazing good,—that is, the stretching did, but the sand scorched our feet like hot embers. Next, we see somebody coming, and started to meet him; but we heard Jim shout, and looked around and he was fairly dancing, and making signs, and yelling. We could n't make out what he said, but we was scared anyway, and begun to heel it back to the balloon. When we got close enough, we understood the words, and they made me sick:

"Run! Run fo' yo' life! Hit 's a lion; I kin see him thoo de glass! Run, boys; do please heel it de bes' you kin. He 's bu'sted outen de menagerie, en dey ain't nobody to stop him!"

It made Tom fly, but it took the stiffening all out of my legs. I could only just gasp along the way you do in a dream when there 's a ghost gaining on you.

Tom got to the ladder and shinned up it a piece and waited for me; and as soon as I got a foothold on it he shouted to Jim to soar away. But Jim had clean lost his head, and said he had forgot how. So Tom shinned along up and told me to follow; but the lion was arriving, fetching a most ghastly roar with every lope, and my legs shook so I das n't try to take one of them out of the rounds for fear the other one would give way under me.

But Tom was aboard by this time, and he started the balloon up a little, and stopped it again as soon as the end of the ladder was ten or twelve feet above ground. And there was the lion, a-ripping around under me, and roaring and springing up in the air at the ladder, and only missing it about a quarter of an inch, it seemed to me. It was delicious to be out of his reach, perfectly delicious, and made me feel good and thankful all up one side; but I was hanging there helpless and could n't climb, and that made me feel perfectly wretched and miserable all down the other. It is most seldom that a person feels so mixed, like that; and it is not to be recommended, either.

Tom asked me what he 'd better do, but I did n't know. He asked me if I could hold on whilst he sailed away to a safe place and left the lion behind. I said I could if he did n't go no higher than he was now; but if he went higher I would lose my head and fall, sure. So he said, "Take a good grip," and he started.

"Don't go so fast," I shouted. "It makes my head swim."

He had started like a lightning express. He slowed down, and we glided over the sand slower, but still in a kind of sickening way; for it *is* uncomfortable to see things sliding and gliding under you like that, and not a sound.

But pretty soon there was plenty of sound, for the lion was catching up. His noise fetched others. You could see them coming on the lope from every direction, and pretty soon there was a couple of dozen of them under me, jumping up at the ladder and snarling and snapping at each other; and so we went skimming along over the sand, and these fellers doing what they could to help us to not forgit the occasion; and then some other beasts come, without an invite, and they started a regular riot down there.

We see this plan was a mistake. We could n't ever git away from them at this gait, and I could n't hold on forever. So Tom took a think, and struck another idea. That was, to kill a lion with the pepper-box revolver, and then sail away while the others stopped to fight over the carcass. So he stopped the balloon still, and done it, and then we sailed off while the fuss was going on, and come down a quarter of a mile off, and they helped me aboard; but by the time we was out of reach again, that gang was on hand once more. And when they see we was really gone and they could n't get us, they sat down on their hams and looked up at us so kind of disappointed that it was as much as a person could do not to see *their* side of the matter.

CHAPTER VI.

IT 'S A CARAVAN.

I was so weak that the only thing I wanted was a chance to lay down, so I made straight for my locker-bunk, and stretched myself out there. But a body could n't get back his strength in no such oven as that, so Tom give the command to soar, and Jim started her aloft.

We had to go up a mile before we struck comfortable weather where it was breezy and pleasant and just right, and pretty soon I was all straight again. Tom had been setting quiet and thinking; but now he jumps up and says:

"I bet you a thousand to one *I* know where we are. We 're in the Great Sahara, as sure as guns!"

He was so excited he could n't hold still; but I was n't. I says:

"Well, then, where 's the Great Sahara? In England or in Scotland?"

"'T ain't in either, it 's in Africa."

Jim's eyes bugged out, and he begun to stare

down with no end of interest, because that was
where his originals come from ; but I did n't
more than half believe it. I could n't, you know ;
it seemed too awful far away for us to have traveled.

But Tom was full of his discovery, as he called
it, and said the lions and the sand meant the
Great Desert, sure. He said he could 'a' found
out, before we sighted land, that we was crowding the land somewheres, if he had thought of one
thing ; and when we asked him what, he said:

"These clocks. They 're chronometers. You
always read about them in sea voyages. One of
them is keeping Grinnage time, and the other is
keeping St. Louis time, like my watch. When
we left St. Louis it was four in the afternoon by
my watch and this clock, and it was ten at night
by this Grinnage clock. Well, at this time of the
year the sun sets about seven o'clock. Now I
noticed the time yesterday evening when the sun
went down, and it was half-past five o'clock by
the Grinnage clock, and half-past eleven A. M. by
my watch and the other clock. You see, the sun
rose and set by my watch in St. Louis, and the
Grinnage clock was six hours fast ; but we 've
come so far east that it comes within less than

"WE SWOOPED DOWN, NOW, ALL OF A SUDDEN."

half an hour of setting by the Grinnage clock, now, and I 'm away out—more than four hours and a half out. You see, that meant that we was closing up on the longitude of Ireland, and would strike it before long if we was p'inted right— which we was n't. No, sir, we 've been a-wandering—wandering 'way down south of east, and it 's my opinion we are in Africa. Look at this map. You see how the shoulder of Africa sticks out to the west. Think how fast we 've traveled ; if we had gone straight east we would be long past England by this time. You watch for noon, all of you, and we 'll stand up, and when we can't cast a shadow we 'll find that this Grinnage clock is coming mighty close to marking twelve. Yes, sir, *I* think we 're in Africa ; and it 's just bully."

Jim was gazing down with the glass. He shook his head and says :

" Mars Tom, I reckon dey 's a mistake som'er's. I hain't seen no niggers yit."

"That 's nothing ; they don't live in the desert. What is that, 'way off yonder ? Gimme a glass."

He took a long look, and said it was like a black string stretched across the sand, but he could n't guess what it was.

"Well," I says, "I reckon maybe you 've got a chance, now, to find out whereabouts this balloon is, because as like as not that is one of these lines here, that 's on the map, that you call meridians of longitude, and we can drop down and look at its number, and—"

"Oh, shucks, Huck Finn, I never see such a lunkhead as you. Did you s'pose there 's meridians of longitude on the *earth ?*"

"Tom Sawyer, they 're set down on the map, and you know it perfectly well, and here they are, and you can see for yourself."

"Of course they 're on the map, but that 's nothing ; there ain't any on the *ground*."

"Tom, do you know that to be so ?"

"Certainly I do."

"Well, then, that map 's a liar again. I never see such a liar as that map."

He fired up at that, and I was ready for him, and Jim was warming his opinion, too, and next minute we 'd 'a' broke loose on another argument, if Tom had n't dropped the glass and begun to clap his hands like a maniac and sing out—

"Camels !—Camels !"

So I grabbed a glass, and Jim, too, and took a look, but I was disappointed, and says—

"Camels your granny, they 're spiders."

"Spiders in a desert, you shad? Spiders walking in a procession? You don't ever reflect, Huck
Finn, and I reckon you really have n't got anything
to reflect *with*. Don't you know we 're as much as
a mile up in the air, and that that string of crawl-
ers is two or three miles away? Spiders, good
land! Spiders as big as a cow? Perhaps you 'd
like to go down and milk one of 'em. But they 're
camels, just the same. It 's a caravan, that 's
what it is, and it 's a mile long."

"Well, then, le' 's go down and look at it. I
don't believe in it, and ain't going to till I see it
and know it."

"All right," he says, and give the command:
"Lower away."

As we come slanting down into the hot
weather, we could see that it was camels, sure
enough, plodding along, an everlasting string of
them, with bales strapped to them, and several
hundred men in long white robes, and a thing
like a shawl bound over their heads and hanging down with tassels and fringes; and some of
the men had long guns and some had n't, and
some was riding and some was walking. And
the weather—well, it was just roasting. And

how slow they did creep along! We swooped
down, now, all of a sudden, and stopped about
a hundred yards over their heads.

The men all set up a yell, and some of them
fell flat on their stomachs, some begun to fire
their guns at us, and the rest broke and scam-
pered every which way, and so did the
camels.

We see that we was making trouble, so we
went up again about a mile, to the cool weather,
and watched them from there. It took them an
hour to get together and form the procession
again; then they started along, but we could see
by the glasses that they was n't paying much attention to anything but us. We poked along,
looking down at them with the glasses, and by
and by we see a big sand mound, and something
like people the other side of it, and there was
something like a man laying on top of the
mound, that raised his head up every now and
then, and seemed to be watching the caravan or
us, we did n't know which. As the caravan got
nearer, he sneaked down on the other side and
rushed to the other men and horses—for that
is what they was—and we see them mount in a
hurry; and next, here they come, like a house

"THE LAST MAN TO GO SNATCHED UP A CHILD, AND CARRIED IT OFF
IN FRONT OF HIM ON HIS HORSE."

afire, some with lances and some with long guns, and all of them yelling the best they could.

They come a-tearing down onto the caravan, and the next minute both sides crashed together and was all mixed up, and there was such another popping of guns as you never heard, and the air got so full of smoke you could only catch glimpses of them struggling together. There must 'a' been six hundred men in that battle, and it was terrible to see. Then they broke up into gangs and groups, fighting tooth and nail, and scurrying and scampering around, and laying into each other like everything ; and whenever the smoke cleared a little you could see dead and wounded people and camels scattered far and wide and all about, and camels racing off in every direction.

At last the robbers see they could n't win, so their chief sounded a signal, and all that was left of them broke away and went scampering across the plain. The last man to go snatched up a child and carried it off in front of him on his horse, and a woman run screaming and begging after him, and followed him away off across the plain till she was separated a long ways from her people ; but it war n't no use, and she had to

give it up, and we see her sink down on the sand
and cover her face with her hands. Then Tom
took the hellum, and started for that yahoo, and
we come a-whizzing down and made a swoop,
and knocked him out of the saddle, child and all;
and he was jarred considerable, but the child
was n't hurt, but laid there working its hands
and legs in the air like a tumble-bug that 's on
its back and can't turn over. The man went
staggering off to overtake his horse, and did n't
know what had hit him, for we was three or four
hundred yards up in the air by this time.

We judged the woman would go and get the
child, now; but she did n't. We could see her,
through the glass, still setting there, with her
head bowed down on her knees; so of course she
had n't seen the performance, and thought her
child was clean gone with the man. She was
nearly a half a mile from her people, so we thought
we might go down to the child, which was about
a quarter of a mile beyond her, and snake it to
her before the caravan people could git to us to
do us any harm; and besides, we reckoned
they had enough business on their hands for one
while, anyway, with the wounded. We thought
we 'd chance it, and we did. We swooped down

" WE COME A-WHIZZING DOWN, MADE A SWOOP, AND KNOCKED HIM OUT
OF THE SADDLE, CHILD AND ALL."

and stopped, and Jim shinned down the ladder and fetched up the kid, which was a nice fat little thing, and in a noble good humor, too, considering it was just out of a battle and been tumbled off of a horse; and then we started for the mother, and stopped back of her and tolerable near by, and Jim slipped down and crept up easy, and when he was close back of her the child googoo'd, the way a child does, and she heard it, and whirled and fetched a shriek of joy, and made a jump for the kid and snatched it and hugged it, and dropped it and hugged Jim, and then snatched off a gold chain and hung it around Jim's neck, and hugged him again, and jerked up the child again, a-sobbing and glorifying all the time ; and Jim he shoved for the ladder and up it, and in a minute we was back up in the sky and the woman was staring up, with the back of her head between her shoulders and the child with its arms locked around her neck. And there she stood, as long as we was in sight a-sailing away in the sky.

CHAPTER VII.

TOM RESPECTS THE FLEA.

"Noon!" says Tom, and so it was. His shadder was just a blot around his feet. We looked, and the Grinnage clock was so close to twelve the difference did n't amount to nothing. So Tom said London was right north of us or right south of us, one or t'other, and he reckoned by the weather and the sand and the camels it was north; and a good many miles north, too; as many as from New York to the city of Mexico, he guessed.

Jim said he reckoned a balloon was a good deal the fastest thing in the world, unless it might be some kinds of birds—a wild pigeon, maybe, or a railroad.

But Tom said he had read about railroads in England going nearly a hundred miles an hour for a little ways, and there never was a bird in the world that could do that—except one, and that was a flea.

"AND WHERE'S YOUR RAILROAD, 'LONGSIDE OF A FLEA?"

"A flea? Why, Mars Tom, in de fust place he ain't a bird, strickly speakin'—"

"He ain't a bird, eh? Well, then, what is he?"

"I don't rightly know, Mars Tom, but I speck he's only jist a' animal. No, I reckon dat won't do, nuther, he ain't big enough for a' animal. He mus' be a bug. Yassir, dat's what he is, he's a bug."

"I bet he ain't, but let it go. What's your second place?"

"Well, in de second place, birds is creturs dat goes a long ways, but a flea don't."

"He don't, don't he? Come, now, what *is* a long distance, if you know?"

"Why, it's miles, and lots of 'em—anybody knows dat."

"Can't a man walk miles?"

"Yassir, he kin."

"As many as a railroad?"

"Yassir, if you give him time."

"Can't a flea?"

"Well,— I s'pose so—ef you gives him heaps of time."

"Now you begin to see, don't you, that *distance* ain't the thing to judge by, at all; it's the time it takes to go the distance *in* that *counts*, ain't it?"

"Well, hit do look sorter so, but I would n't 'a' b'lieved it, Mars Tom."

"It 's a matter of *proportion*, that 's what it is; and when you come to gauge a thing's speed by its size, where 's your bird and your man and your railroad, alongside of a flea? The fastest man can't run more than about ten miles in an hour—not much over ten thousand times his own length. But all the books says any common ordinary third-class flea can jump a hundred and fifty times his own length; yes, and he can make five jumps a second too,—seven hundred and fifty times his own length, in one little second— for he don't fool away any time stopping and starting—he does them both at the same time; you 'll see, if you try to put your finger on him. Now that 's a common, ordinary, third-class flea's gait; but you take an Eyetalian *first*-class, that 's been the pet of the nobility all his life, and has n't ever knowed what want or sickness or exposure was, and he can jump more than three hundred times his own length, and keep it up all day, five such jumps every second, which is fifteen hundred times his own length. Well, suppose a man could go fifteen hundred times his own length in a second—say, a mile and a half. It 's

ninety miles a minute; it 's considerable more
than five thousand miles an hour. Where 's
your man *now?*—yes, and your bird, and your
railroad, and your balloon? Laws, they don't
amount to shucks 'longside of a flea. A flea is
just a comet b'iled down small."

Jim was a good deal astonished, and so was I.
Jim said—

" Is dem figgers jist edjackly true, en no jokin'
en no lies, Mars Tom?"

" Yes, they are; they 're perfectly true."

" Well, den, honey, a body 's got to respec' a
flea. I ain't had no respec' for um befo', sca'sely,
but dey ain't no gittin' roun' it, dey do deserve
it, dat 's certain."

" Well, I bet they do. They 've got ever so
much more sense, and brains, and brightness, in
proportion to their size, than any other cretur in
the world. A person can learn them 'most anything; and they learn it quicker than any other
cretur, too. They 've been learnt to haul little
carriages in harness, and go this way and that
way and t' other way according to their orders;
yes, and to march and drill like soldiers, doing
it as exact, according to orders, as soldiers does
it. They 've been learnt to do all sorts of hard

and troublesome things. S'pose you could culti-
vate a flea up to the size of a man, and keep his
natural smartness a-growing and a-growing right
along up, bigger and bigger, and keener and
keener, in the same proportion—where 'd the
human race be, do you reckon? That flea would
be President of the United States, and you
could n't any more prevent it than you can prevent lightning."

"My lan', Mars Tom, I never knowed dey was
so much *to* de beas'. No, sir, I never had no
idea of it, and dat 's de fac'."

"There 's more to him, by a long sight, than
there is to any other cretur, man or beast, in proportion to size. He's the interestingest of them
all. People have so much to say about an ant's
strength, and an elephant's, and a locomotive's.
Shucks, they don't begin with a flea. He can
lift two or three hundred times his own weight.
And none of them can come anywhere near it.
And moreover, he has got notions of his own,
and is very particular, and you can't fool him;
his instinct, or his judgment, or whatever it is, is
perfectly sound and clear, and don't ever make a
mistake. People think all humans are alike to a
flea. It ain't so. There 's folks that he won't go

near, hungry or not hungry, and I 'm one of
them.   I 've never had one of them on me in my
life."

"Mars Tom !"

"It 's so ; I ain't joking."

"Well, sah, I hain't ever heard de likes o' dat,
befo'."

Jim could n't believe it, and I could n't ; so
we had to drop down to the sand and git a supply and see. Tom was right. They went for
me and Jim by the thousand, but not a one of
them lit on Tom.   There war n't no explaining
it, but there it was and there war n't no getting
around it.   He said it had always been just so,
and he 'd just as soon be where there was a million of them as not ; they 'd never touch him
nor bother him.

We went up to the cold weather to freeze 'em
out, and stayed a little spell, and then come
back to the comfortable weather and went lazy-
ing along twenty or twenty-five miles an hour,
the way we 'd been doing for the last few hours.
The reason was, that the longer we was in that
solemn, peaceful desert, the more the hurry and
fuss got kind of soothed down in us, and the
more happier and contented and satisfied we

got to feeling, and the more we got to liking
the desert, and then loving it. So we had
cramped the speed down, as I was saying, and
was having a most noble good lazy time, sometimes watching through the glasses, sometimes
stretched out on the lockers reading, sometimes
taking a nap.

It did n't seem like we was the same lot that
was in such a state to find land and git ashore,
but it was. But we had got over that—clean
over it. We was used to the balloon, now, and
not afraid any more, and did n't want to be any-
wheres else. Why, it seemed just like home ; it
'most seemed as if I had been born and raised
in it, and Jim and Tom said the same. And
always I had had hateful people around me,
a-nagging at me, and pestering of me, and scolding, and finding fault, and fussing and bothering, and sticking to me, and keeping after me,
and making me do this, and making me do that
and t'other, and always selecting out the things
I did n't want to do, and then giving me Sam
Hill because I shirked and done something else,
and just aggravating the life out of a body all
the time ; but up here in the sky it was so still
and sunshiny and lovely, and plenty to eat, and

"WHERE'S YOUR MAN NOW?"

plenty of sleep, and strange things to see, and no nagging and no pestering, and no good people, and just holiday all the time. Land, I war n't in no hurry to git out and buck at civilization again. Now, one of the worst things about civilization is, that anybody that gits a letter with trouble in it comes and tells you all about it and makes you feel bad, and the newspapers fetches you the troubles of everybody all over the world, and keeps you down-hearted and dismal 'most all the time, and it 's such a heavy load for a person. I hate them newspapers; and I hate letters; and if I had my way I would n't allow nobody to load his troubles onto other folks he ain't acquainted with, on t'other side of the world, that way. Well, up in a balloon there ain't any of that, and it 's the darlingest place there is.

We had supper, and that night was one of the prettiest nights I ever see. The moon made it just like daylight, only a heap softer; and once we see a lion standing all alone by himself, just all alone on the earth, it seemed like, and his shadder laid on the sand by him like a puddle of ink. That 's the kind of moonlight to have.

Mainly we laid on our backs and talked; we

did n't want to go to sleep. Tom said we was right in the midst of the Arabian Nights, now. He said it was right along here that one of the cutest things in that book happened; so we looked down and watched while he told about it, because there ain't anything that is so interesting to look at as a place that a book has talked about. It was a tale about a camel-driver that had lost his camel, and he come along in the desert and met a man, and says—

"Have you run across a stray camel to-day?"

And the man says—

"Was he blind in his left eye?"

"Yes."

"Had he lost an upper front tooth?"

"Yes."

"Was his off hind leg lame?"

"Yes."

"Was he loaded with millet-seed on one side and honey on the other?"

"Yes, but you need n't go into no more details—that 's the one, and I 'm in a hurry. Where did you see him?"

"I hain't seen him at all," the man says.

"Hain't seen him at all? How can you describe him so close, then?"

"THAT FLEA WOULD BE PRESIDENT OF THE UNITED STATES, AND YOU COULD NOT PREVENT IT."

"Because when a person knows how to use his eyes, everything has got a meaning to it; but most people's eyes ain't any good to them. I knowed a camel had been along, because I seen his track. I knowed he was lame in his off hind leg because he had favored that foot and trod light on it, and his track showed it. I knowed he was blind on his left side because he only nibbled the grass on the right side of the trail. I knowed he had lost an upper front tooth because where he bit into the sod his teeth-print showed it. The millet-seed sifted out on one side—the ants told me that; the honey leaked out on the other—the flies told me that. I know all about your camel, but I hain't seen him."

Jim says—

"Go on, Mars Tom, hit 's a mighty good tale, and powerful interestin'."

"That 's all," Tom says.

"*All?*" says Jim, astonished. "What 'come o' de camel?"

"I don't know."

"Mars Tom, don't de tale say?"

"No."

Jim puzzled a minute, then he says—

"Well! Ef dat ain't de beatenes' tale ever *I* struck. Jist gits to de place whah de intrust is gittin' red-hot, en down she breaks. Why, Mars Tom, dey ain't no *sense* in a tale dat acts like dat. Hain't you got no *idea* whether de man got de camel back er not?"

"No, I have n't."

I see, myself, there war n't no sense in the tale, to chop square off, that way, before it come to anything, but I war n't going to say so, because I could see Tom was souring up pretty fast over the way it flatted out and the way Jim had popped onto the weak place in it, and I don't think it 's fair for everybody to pile onto a feller when he 's down. But Tom he whirls on me and says—

" What do *you* think of the tale?"

Of course, then, I had to come out and make a clean breast and say it did seem to me, too, same as it did to Jim, that as long as the tale stopped square in the middle and never got to no place, it really war n't worth the trouble of telling.

Tom's chin dropped on his breast, and 'stead of being mad, as I reckoned he 'd be, to hear me scoff at his tale that way, he seemed to be only sad ; and he says—

"Some people can see, and some can't—just as that man said. Let alone a camel, if a cyclone had gone by, *you* duffers would n't 'a' noticed the track."

I don't know what he meant by that, and he did n't say ; it was just one of his irrulevances, I reckon—he was full of them, sometimes, when he was in a close place and could n't see no other way out—but I did n't mind. We 'd spotted the soft place in that tale sharp enough, he could n't git away from that little fact. It graveled him like the nation, too, I reckon, much as he tried not to let on.

CHAPTER VIII.

THE DISAPPEARING LAKE.

WE had an early breakfast in the morning, and set looking down on the desert, and the weather was ever so bammy and lovely, although we war n't high up. You have to come down lower and lower after sundown, in the desert, because it cools off so fast; and so, by the time it is getting towards dawn you are skimming along only a little ways above the sand.

We was watching the shadder of the balloon slide along the ground, and now and then gazing off across the desert to see if anything was stirring, and then down at the shadder again, when all of a sudden almost right under us we see a lot of men and camels laying scattered about, perfectly quiet, like they was asleep.

We shut off the power, and backed up and stood over them, and then we see that they was all dead. It give us the cold shivers. And it made us hush down, too, and talk low, like people at a funeral. We dropped down slow, and stopped, and me and Tom clumb down and went amongst them. There was men, and women, and children. They was dried by the sun and dark and shriveled and leathery, like the pictures of mummies you see in books. And yet they looked just as human, you would n't 'a' believed it ; just like they was asleep.

Some of the people and animals was partly covered with sand, but most of them not, for the sand was thin there, and the bed was gravel, and hard. Most of the clothes had rotted away ; and when you took hold of a rag, it tore with a touch, like spider-web. Tom reckoned they had been laying there for years.

Some of the men had rusty guns by them, some had swords on and had shawl belts with long silver-mounted pistols stuck in them. All the camels had their loads on, yet, but the packs had busted or rotted and spilt the freight out on the ground. We did n't reckon the swords was any good to the dead people any more, so we took one apiece, and some pistols. We took a small box, too, because it was so handsome and inlaid so fine ; and then we wanted to bury the people ; but there war n't no way to do it that we could think of, and nothing to do it with but sand, and that would blow away again, of course.

Then we mounted high and sailed away, and pretty soon that black spot on the sand was out of sight and we would n't ever see them poor people again in this world. We wondered, and reasoned, and tried to guess how they come to be there, and how it all happened to them, but we could n't make it out. First we thought maybe they got lost, and wandered around and about till their food and water give out and they starved to death ; but Tom said no wild animals nor vultures had n't meddled with them, and so that guess would n't do. So at last we give it up, and judged we would n't think about it no more, because it made us low-spirited.

Then we opened the box, and it had gems and jewels in it, quite a pile, and some little veils of the kind the dead women had on, with fringes made out of curious gold money that we war n't acquainted with. We wondered if we better go and try to find them again and give it back ; but Tom thought it over and said no, it was a country that was full of robbers, and they would come and steal it, and then the sin would be on us for putting the temptation in their way. So

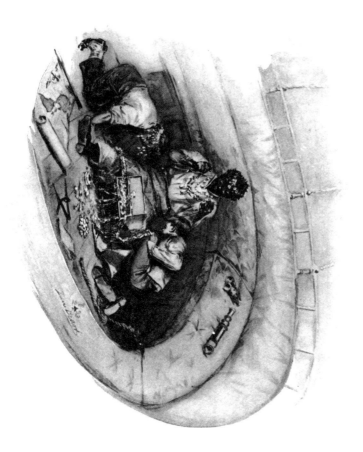

"WE OPENED THE BOX, AND IT HAD GEMS AND JEWELS IN IT."

we went on ; but I wished we had took all they had, so there would n't 'a' been no temptation at all left.

We had had two hours of that blazing weather down there, and was dreadful thirsty when we got aboard again. We went straight for the water, but it was spoiled and bitter, besides being pretty near hot enough to scald your mouth. We could n't drink it. It was Mississippi river water, the best in the world, and we stirred up the mud in it to see if that would help, but no, the mud was n't any better than the water.

Well, we had n't been so very, very thirsty before, whilst we was interested in the lost people, but we was, now, and as soon as we found we could n't have a drink, we was more than thirty-five times as thirsty as we was a quarter of a minute before. Why, in a little while we wanted to hold our mouths open and pant like a dog.

Tom said to keep a sharp lookout, all around, everywheres, because we 'd got to find an oasis or there war n't no telling what would happen. So we done it. We kept the glasses gliding around all the time, till our arms got so tired we could n't hold them any more. Two hours—

three hours—just gazing and gazing, and nothing but sand, sand, *sand*, and you could see the
quivering heat-shimmer playing over it. Dear,
dear, a body don't know what real misery is till
he is thirsty all the way through and is certain
he ain't ever going to come to any water any
more. At last I could n't stand it to look around
on them baking plains; I laid down on the
locker, and give it up.

But by and by Tom raised a whoop, and there
she was! A lake, wide and shiny, with pam-
trees leaning over it asleep, and their shadders
in the water just as soft and delicate as ever you
see. I never see anything look so good. It was
a long ways off, but that war n't anything to us;
we just slapped on a hundred-mile gait, and cal-
culated to be there in seven minutes; but she
stayed the same old distance away, all the time;
we could n't seem to gain on her; yes, sir, just
as far, and shiny, and like a dream; but we
could n't get no nearer; and at last, all of a sudden, she was gone!

Tom's eyes took a spread, and he says—

" Boys, it was a *my*ridge!" Said it like he was
glad. I did n't see nothing to be glad about. I
says—

"May be. I don't care nothing about its name, the thing I want to know is, what 's become of it?"

Jim was trembling all over, and so scared he could n't speak, but he wanted to ask that question himself if he could 'a' done it. Tom says—

"What 's *become* of it? Why, you see, yourself, it 's gone."

"Yes, I know; but where 's it gone *to?*"

He looked me over and says—

"Well, now, Huck Finn, where *would* it go to? Don't you know what a myridge is?"

"No, I don't. What is it?"

"It ain't anything but imagination. There ain't anything *to* it."

It warmed me up a little to hear him talk like that, and I says—

"What 's the use you talking that kind of stuff, Tom Sawyer? Did n't I see the lake?"

"Yes—you think you did."

"I don't think nothing about it, I *did* see it."

"I tell you you *did n't* see it either—because it war n't there to see."

It astonished Jim to hear him talk so, and he broke in and says, kind of pleading and distressed—

"Mars Tom, *please* don't say sich things in sich an awful time as dis.   You ain't only reskin' yo' own self, but you 's reskin' us — same way like Anna Nias en' Siffira.   De lake *wuz* dah—I seen it jis' as plain as I sees you en Huck dis minute."

I says—

"Why, he seen it himself!   He was the very one that seen it first.   *Now*, then!"

"Yes, Mars Tom, hit 's so — you can't deny it.   We all seen it, en dat *prove* it was dah."

"Proves it!   *How* does it prove it?"

"Same way it does in de courts en everywheres, Mars Tom.   One pusson might be drunk, or dreamy or suthin', en he could be mistaken; en two might, maybe; but I tell you, sah, when three sees a thing, drunk er sober, it 's *so*.   Dey ain't no gittin' aroun' dat, en you knows it, Mars Tom."

"I don't know nothing of the kind.   There used to be forty thousand million people that seen the sun move from one side of the sky to the other every day.   Did that prove that the sun *done* it?"

"'Course it did.   En besides, dey war n't no 'casion to prove it.   A body 'at 's got any sense ain't gwine to doubt it.   Dah she is, now — a sailin' thoo de sky, like she allays done."

Tom turned on me, then, and says—

" What do *you* say—is the sun standing still ? "

" Tom Sawyer, what 's the use to ask such a jackass question ?   Anybody that ain't blind can see it don't stand still."

" Well," he says, " I 'm lost in the sky with no company but a passel of low-down animals that don't know no more than the head boss of a university did three or four hundred years ago."

It war n't fair play, and I let him know it.   I says—

" Throwin' mud ain't arguin', Tom Sawyer."

" Oh, my goodness, oh, my goodness gracious, dah 's de lake ag'in!" yelled Jim, just then. " *Now*, Mars Tom, what you gwine to say ? "

Yes, sir, there was the lake again, away yonder across the desert, perfectly plain, trees and all, just the same as it was before.   I says—

" I reckon you 're satisfied now, Tom Sawyer."

But he says, perfectly ca'm—

" Yes, satisfied there ain't no lake there."

Jim says—

" *Don't* talk so, Mars Tom—it sk'yers me to hear you.   It 's so hot, en you 's so thirsty, dat

you ain't in yo' right mine, Mars Tom. Oh,
but don't she look good! 'clah I doan' know
how I 's gwine to wait tell we gits dah, I 's *so*
thirsty."

"Well, you 'll have to wait; and it won't do
you no good, either, because there ain't no lake
there, I tell you."

I says—

"Jim, don't you take your eye off of it, and
I won't, either."

"'Deed I won't; en bless you, honey, I
could n't ef I wanted to."

We went a-tearing along toward it, piling the
miles behind us like nothing, but never gaining
an inch on it—and all of a sudden it was gone
again! Jim staggered, and 'most fell down.
When he got his breath he says, gasping like a
fish—

"Mars Tom, hit 's a *ghos*', dat 's what it is, en
I hopes to goodness we ain't gwine to see it no
mo'. Dey 's *been* a lake, en suthin 's happened,
en de lake 's dead, en we 's seen its ghos'; we 's
seen it twiste, en dat 's proof. De desert 's
ha'nted, it 's ha'nted, sho'; oh, Mars Tom, le's git
outen it; I 'd ruther die den have de night ketch
us in it ag'in en de ghos' er dat lake come

a-mournin' aroun' us en we asleep en doan' know de danger we 's in."

"Ghost, you gander! It ain't anything but air and heat and thirstiness pasted together by a person's imagination. If I—gimme the glass!"

He grabbed it and begun to gaze off to the right.

" It 's a flock of birds," he says. " It 's getting toward sundown, and they 're making a bee-line across our track for somewheres. They mean business—maybe they 're going for food or water, or both. Let her go to starboard!—Port your hellum! Hard down! There—ease up—steady, as you go."

We shut down some of the power, so as not to outspeed them, and took out after them. We went skimming along a quarter of a mile behind them, and when we had followed them an hour and a half and was getting pretty discouraged, and was thirsty clean to unendurableness, Tom says—

"Take the glass, one of you, and see what that is, away ahead of the birds."

Jim got the first glimpse, and slumped down on the locker, sick. He was most crying, and says—

"She's dah agi'n, Mars Tom, she's dah ag'in, en I knows I's gwine to die, 'case when a body sees a ghos' de third time, dat's what it means. I wisht I'd never come in dis balloon, dat I does."

He would n't look no more, and what he said made me afraid, too, because I knowed it was true, for that has always been the way with ghosts; so then I would n't look any more, either. Both of us begged Tom to turn off and go some other way, but he would n't, and said we was ignorant superstitious blatherskites. Yes, and he 'll git come up with, one of these days, I says to myself, insulting ghosts that way. They 'll stand it for a while, maybe, but they won't stand it always, for anybody that knows about ghosts knows how easy they are hurt, and how revengeful they are.

So we was all quiet and still, Jim and me being scared, and Tom busy. By and by Tom fetched the balloon to a standstill, and says—

"*Now* get up and look, you sapheads."

We done it, and there was the sure-enough water right under us!—clear, and blue, and cool, and deep, and wavy with the breeze, the loveliest sight that ever was. And all about it was

grassy banks, and flowers, and shady groves of
big trees, looped together with vines, and all
looking so peaceful and comfortable, enough to
make a body cry, it was so beautiful.

Jim *did* cry, and rip and dance and carry on,
he was so thankful and out of his mind for joy.
It was my watch, so I had to stay by the works,
but Tom and Jim clumb down and drunk a bar-
rel apiece, and fetched me up a lot, and I 've
tasted a many a good thing in my life, but nothing that ever begun with that water.

Then we went down and had a swim, and then
Tom came up and spelled me, and me and Jim
had a swim, and then Jim spelled Tom, and me
and Tom had a foot-race and a boxing-mill, and
I don't reckon I ever had such a good time in
my life. It war n't so very hot, because it was
close on to evening, and we had n't any clothes
on, anyway. Clothes is well enough in school,
and in towns, and at balls, too, but there ain't no
sense in them when there ain't no civilization
nor other kinds of bothers and fussiness around.

"Lions a-comin'!—lions! Quick, Mars Tom,
jump for yo' life, Huck!"

Oh, and did n't we! We never stopped for
clothes, but waltzed up the ladder just so. Jim

lost his head straight off—he always done it whenever he got excited and scared; and so now, 'stead of just easing the ladder up from the ground a little, so the animals could n't reach it, he turned on a raft of power, and we went whizzing up and was dangling in the sky before he got his wits together and seen what a foolish thing he was doing. Then he stopped her, but he had clean forgot what to do next; so there we was, so high that the lions looked like pups, and we was drifting off on the wind.

But Tom he shinned up and went for the works and begun to slant her down, and back towards the lake, where the animals was gathering like a camp-meeting, and I judged he had lost *his* head, too; for he knowed I was too scared to climb, and did he want to dump me among the tigers and things?

But no, his head was level, he knowed what he was about. He swooped down to within thirty or forty feet of the lake, and stopped right over the centre, and sung out—

"Leggo, and drop!"

I done it, and shot down, feet first, and seemed to go about a mile toward the bottom; and when I come up, he says—

"AND ALL THIS TIME THE LIONS AND TIGERS WAS SORTING OUT THE CLOTHES."

" Now lay on your back and float till you 're
rested and got your pluck back, then I 'll dip the
ladder in the water and you can climb aboard."

I done it. Now that was ever so smart in
Tom, because if he had started off somewheres
else to drop down on the sand, the menagerie
would 'a' come along, too, and might 'a' kept us
hunting a safe place till I got tuckered out and fell.

And all this time the lions and tigers was sorting out the clothes, and trying to divide them
up so there would be some for all, but there was
a misunderstanding about it somewheres, on accounts of some of them trying to hog more than
their share ; so there was another insurrection,
and you never see anything like it in the world.
There must 'a' been fifty of them, all mixed up
together, snorting and roaring and snapping and
biting and tearing, legs and tails in the air and
you could n't tell which was which, and the sand
and fur a-flying. And when they got done,
some was dead, and some was limping off crippled, and the rest was setting around on the bat-
tle-field, some of them licking their sore places
and the others looking up at us and seemed to
be kind of inviting us to come down and have
some fun, but which we did n't want any.

As for the clothes, they war n't any, any more.
Every last rag of them was inside of the animals ; and not agreeing with them very well, I
don't reckon, for there was considerable many
brass buttons on them, and there was knives in
the pockets, too, and smoking-tobacco, and nails
and chalk and marbles and fish-hooks and
things. But I was n't caring. All that was
bothering me was, that all we had, now, was the
professor's clothes, a big enough assortment, but
not suitable to go into company with, if we
came across any, because the britches was as
long as tunnels, and the coats and things according. Still, there was everything a tailor needed,
and Jim was a kind of jack-legged tailor, and he
allowed he could soon trim a suit or two down
for us that would answer.

CHAPTER IX.

TOM DISCOURSES ON THE DESERT.

STILL, we thought we would drop down there a minute, but on another errand. Most of the professor's cargo of food was put up in cans, in the new way that somebody had just invented, the rest was fresh. When you fetch Missouri beefsteak to the Great Sahara, you want to be particular and stay up in the coolish weather. So we reckoned we would drop down into the lion market and see how we could make out there.

We hauled in the ladder and dropped down till we was just above the reach of the animals, then we let down a rope with a slip-knot in it and hauled up a dead lion, a small tender one, then yanked up a cub tiger. We had to keep the congregation off with the revolver, or they would 'a' took a hand in the proceedings and helped.

We carved off a supply from both, and saved

the skins, and hove the rest overboard. Then we baited some of the professor's hooks with the fresh meat and went a-fishing. We stood over the lake just a convenient distance above the water, and catched a lot of the nicest fish you ever see. It was a most amazing good supper we had ; lion steak, tiger steak, fried fish and hot corn pone. I don't want nothing better than that.

We had some fruit to finish off with. We got it out of the top of a monstrous tall tree. It was a very slim tree that had n't a branch on it from the bottom plumb to the top, and there it busted out like a feather-duster. It was a pam tree, of course ; anybody knows a pam tree the minute he see it, by the pictures. We went for coconuts in this one, but there war n't none. There was only big loose bunches of things like over-sized grapes, and Tom allowed they was dates, because he said they answered the description in the Arabian Nights and the other books. Of course they might n't be, and they might be pison ; so we had to wait a spell, and watch and see if the birds et them. They done it ; so we done it too, and they was most amazing good.

By this time monstrous big birds begun to

come and settle on the dead animals. They was
plucky creturs ; they would tackle one end of a
lion that was being gnawed at the other end by
another lion. If the lion drove the bird away,
it did n't do no good, he was back again the
minute the lion was busy.

The big birds come out of every part of the
sky—you could make them out with the glass
whilst they was still so far away you could n't
see them with your naked eye. Tom said the
birds did n't find out the meat was there by the
smell, they had to find it out by seeing it. Oh,
but ain't that an eye for you ! Tom said at the
distance of five mile a patch of dead lions
could n't look any bigger than a person's finger
nail, and he could n't imagine how the birds
could notice such a little thing so far off.

It was strange and unnatural to see lion eat
lion, and we thought maybe they war n't kin.
But Jim said that did n't make no difference.
He said a hog was fond of her own children, and
so was a spider, and he reckoned maybe a lion
was pretty near as unprincipled though maybe
not quite. He thought likely a lion would n't eat
his own father, if he knowed which was him, but
reckoned he would eat his brother-in-law if he

was uncommon hungry, and eat his mother-in-
law any time. But *reckoning* don't settle nothing. You can reckon till the cows come home,
but that don't fetch you to no decision. So we
give it up and let it drop.

Generly it was very still in the Desert, nights,
but this time there was music. A lot of other
animals come to dinner ; sneaking yelpers that
Tom allowed was jackals, and roached-backed
ones that he said was hyenas ; and all the whole
biling of them kept up a racket all the time.
They made a picture in the moonlight that was
more different than any picture I ever see. We
had a line out and made fast to the top of a tree,
and did n't stand no watch, but all turned in and
slept, but I was up two or three times to look
down at the animals and hear the music. It was
like having a front seat at a menagerie for nothing, which I had n't ever had before, and so it
seemed foolish to sleep and not make the most
of it, I might n't ever have such a chance again.

We went a-fishing again in the early dawn,
and then lazied around all day in the deep shade
on an island, taking turn about to watch and
see that none of the animals come a-snooping
around there after erronorts for dinner. We

was going to leave the next day, but could n't, it was too lovely.

The day after, when we rose up toward the sky and sailed off eastward, we looked back and watched that place till it war n't nothing but just a speck in the Desert, and I tell you it was like saying good-by to a friend that you ain't ever going to see any more.

Jim was thinking to himself, and at last he says—

"Mars Tom, we 's mos' to de end er de Desert now, I speck."

"Why ?"

"Well, hit stan' to reason we is. You knows how long we 's been a-skimmin' over it. Mus' be mos' out o' san'. Hit 's a wonder to me dat it 's hilt out as long as it has."

"Shucks, there 's plenty sand, you need n't worry."

"Oh, I ain't a-worryin', Mars Tom, only wonderin', dat 's all. De Lord 's got plenty san' I ain't doubtin' dat, but nemmine, He ain' gwyne to *was'e* it jist on dat account ; en I allows dat dis Desert 's plenty big enough now, jist de way she is, en you can't spread her out no mo' 'dout was'in san'."

"Oh, go 'long! we ain't much more than fairly *started* across this Desert yet. The United States is a pretty big country, ain't it? Ain't it, Huck?"

"Yes," I says "there ain't no bigger one, I don't reckon."

"Well," he says, "this Desert is about the shape of the United States, and if you was to lay it down on top of the United States, it would cover the land of the free out of sight like a blanket. There 'd be a little corner sticking out, up at Maine and away up northwest, and Florida sticking out like a turtle's tail, and that 's all. We 've took California away from the Mexicans two or three years ago, so that part of the Pacific coast is ours, now, and if you laid the Great Sahara down with her edge on the Pacific, she would cover the United States and stick out past New York six hundred miles into the Atlantic Ocean."

I says—

"Good land! have you got the documents for that, Tom Sawyer?"

"Yes, and they 're right here, and I 've been studying them. You can look for yourself. From New York to the Pacific is 2,600 miles.

From one end of the Great Desert to the other
is 3,200. The United States contains 3,600,000
square miles, the Desert contains 4,162,000.
With the Desert's bulk you could cover up every
last inch of the United States, and in under
where the edges projected out, you could tuck
England, Scotland, Ireland, France, Denmark, and
all Germany. Yes, sir, you could hide the home
of the brave and all of them countries clean out
of sight under the Great Sahara, and you would
still have 2,000 square miles of sand left."

"Well," I says, "it clean beats me. Why,
Tom, it shows that the Lord took as much pains
makin' this Desert as makin' the United States
and all them other countries."

Jim says—"Huck, dat don' stan' to reason. I
reckon dis Desert wa' n't made, at all. Now you
take en look at it like dis—you look at it, and
see ef I 's right. What 's a desert good for?
'T ain't good for nuthin'. Dey ain't no way to
make it pay. Hain't dat so, Huck?"

"Yes, I reckon."

"Hain't it so, Mars Tom?"

"I guess so. Go on."

"Ef a thing ain't no good, it 's made in vain,
ain't it?"

" Yes."

"*Now*, den! Do de Lord make anything in vain? You answer me dat."

" Well—no, He don't."

" Den how come He make a desert?"

" Well, go on. How *did* He come to make it?"

" Mars Tom, *I* b'lieve it uz jes like when you 's buildin' a house; dey 's allays a lot o' truck en rubbish lef' over. What does you do wid it? Doan' you take en k'yart it off en dump it into a ole vacant back lot? 'Course. Now, den, it 's my opinion hit was jes like dat—dat de Great Sahara war n't made at all, she jes *happen'*."

I said it was a real good argument, and I believed it was the best one Jim ever made. Tom he said the same, but said the trouble about arguments is, they ain't nothing but *theories*, after all, and theories don't prove nothing, they only give you a place to rest on, a spell, when you are tuckered out butting around and around trying to find out something there ain't no way *to* find out. And he says—

" There 's another trouble about theories: there 's always a hole in them somewheres, sure, if you look close enough. It 's just so with this

one of Jim's.   Look what billions and billions of
stars there is.   How does it come that there was
just exactly enough star-stuff, and none left
over?   How does it come there ain't no sand-
pile up there?"

But Jim was fixed for him and says—

"What's de Milky Way?—dat's what *I* wants
to know.   What's de Milky Way?   Answer
me dat!"

In my opinion it was just a sockdologer.   It's
only an opinion, it's only *my* opinion and others
may think different; but I said it then and I
stand to it now—it was a sockdologer.   And
moreover, besides, it landed Tom Sawyer.   He
could n't say a word.   He had that stunned look
of a person that 's been shot in the back with a
kag of nails.   All he said was, as for people like
me and Jim, he 'd just as soon have intellectual
intercourse with a catfish.   But anybody can say
that—and I notice they always do, when somebody has fetched them a lifter.   Tom Sawyer
was tired of that end of the subject.

So we got back to talking about the size of
the Desert again, and the more we compared it
with this and that and t' other thing, the more
nobler and bigger and grander it got to look,

right along. And so, hunting amongst the figgers, Tom found, by and by, that it was just
the same size as the Empire of China. Then he
showed us the spread the Empire of China made
on the map, and the room she took up in the
world. Well, it was wonderful to think of, and
I says—

"Why, I 've heard talk about this Desert plenty
of times, but *I* never knowed, before, how important she was."

Then Tom says—

"Important! Sahara important! That 's just
the way with some people. If a thing 's big,
it 's important. That 's all the sense they 've
got. All they can see is *size*. Why, look at
England. It 's the most important country in
the world; and yet you could put it in China's
vest pocket; and not only that, but you 'd have
the dickens's own time to find it again the next
time you wanted it. And look at Russia. It
spreads all around and everywhere, and yet ain't
no more important in this world than Rhode
Island is, and has n't got half as much in it
that 's worth saving."

Away off, now, we see a little hill, a-standing
up just on the edge of the world. Tom broke

off his talk, and reached for a glass very much excited, and took a look, and says—

"That 's it—it 's the one I 've been looking for, sure. If I 'm right, it 's the one the Dervish took the man into and showed him all the treasures."

So we begun to gaze, and he begun to tell about it out of the Arabian Nights.

CHAPTER X.

THE TREASURE-HILL.

Tom said it happened like this.

A dervish was stumping it along through the desert, on foot, one blazing hot day, and he had come a thousand miles and was pretty poor, and hungry, and ornery and tired, and along about where we are now, he run across a camel driver with a hundred camels, and asked him for some ams. But the camel driver he asked to be excused. The dervish says—

" Don't you own these camels ? "

" Yes, they 're mine."

" Are you in debt ? "

" Who—me ? No."

" Well, a man that owns a hundred camels and ain't in debt, is rich—and not only rich, but very rich. Ain't it so ? "

The camel driver owned up that it was so. Then the dervish says—

" God has made you rich, and He has made me poor. He has His reasons, and they are wise, blessed be His name. But He has willed that

His rich shall help His poor, and you have turned away from me, your brother, in my need, and He will remember this, and you will lose by it."

That made the camel driver feel shaky, but all the same he was born hoggish after money and did n't like to let go a cent, so he begun to whine and explain, and said times was hard, and although he had took a full freight down to Balsora and got a fat rate for it, he could n't git no return freight, and so he war n't making no great things out of his trip. So the dervish starts along again, and says—

"All right, if you want to take the risk, but I reckon you 've made a mistake this time, and missed a chance."

Of course the camel driver wanted to know what kind of a chance he had missed, because maybe there was money in it ; so he run after the dervish and begged him so hard and earnest to take pity on him and tell him, that at last the dervish give in, and says—

"Do you see that hill yonder? Well, in that hill is all the treasures of the earth, and I was looking around for a man with a particular good kind heart and a noble generous disposition, because if I could find just that man, I 've got a kind of a salve I could put on his eyes and he could see the treasures and get them out."

So then the camel driver was in a sweat; and he cried, and begged, and took on, and went down on his knees, and said he was just that kind of a man, and said he could fetch a thousand people that would say he was n't ever described so exact before.

"Well, then," says the dervish, "all right. If we load the hundred camels, can I have half of them?"

The driver was so glad he could n't hardly hold in, and says—

"Now you 're shouting."

So they shook hands on the bargain, and the dervish got out his box and rubbed the salve on the driver's right eye, and the hill opened and he went in, and there, sure enough, was piles and piles of gold and jewels sparkling like all the stars in heaven had fell down.

So him and the dervish laid into it and they loaded every camel till he could n't carry no more, then they said good-by, and each of them started off with his fifty. But pretty soon the camel driver come a-running and overtook the dervish and says—

"You ain't in society, you know, and you don't

THE CAMEL-DRIVER IN THE TREASURE-CAVE.

really need all you 've got. Won't you be good, and let me have ten of your camels?"

"Well," the dervish says, "I don't know but what you say is reasonable enough."

So he done it, and they separated and the dervish started off again with his forty. But pretty soon here comes the camel driver bawling after him again, and whines and slobbers around and begs another ten off of him, saying thirty camel loads of treasures was enough to see a dervish through, because they live very simple, you know, and don't keep house but board around and give their note.

But that war n't the end, yet. That ornery hound kept coming and coming till he had begged back all the camels and had the whole hundred. Then he was satisfied, and ever so grateful, and said he would n't ever forget the dervish as long as he lived, and nobody had n't ever been so good to him before, and liberal. So they shook hands good-by, and separated and started off again.

But do you know, it war n't ten minutes till the camel driver was unsatisfied again—he was the low-downest reptyle in seven counties—and he come a-running again. And this time the

thing he wanted was to get the dervish to rub
some of the salve on his other eye.

"Why?" said the dervish.

"Oh, you know," says the driver.

"Know what?"

"Well, you can't fool me," says the driver.
"You 're trying to keep back something from
me, you know it mighty well. You know, I
reckon, that if I had the salve on the other eye I
could see a lot more things that 's valuable.
Come—please put it on."

The dervish says—

"I was n't keeping anything back from you.
I don't mind telling you what would happen if
I put it on. You 'd never see again. You 'd be
stone blind the rest of your days."

But do you know, that beat would n't believe
him. No, he begged and begged, and whined
and cried, till at last the dervish opened his box
and told him to put it on, if he wanted to. So
the man done it, and sure enough he was as blind
as a bat, in a minute.

Then the dervish laughed at him and mocked
at him and made fun of him ; and says—

"Good-by—a man that 's blind hain't got no
use for jewelry."

And he cleared out with the hundred camels, and left that man to wander around poor and miserable and friendless the rest of his days in the desert.

Jim said he 'd bet it was a lesson to him.

"Yes," Tom says, "and like a considerable many lessons a body gets. They ain't no account, because the thing don't ever happen the same way again — and can't. The time Hen Scovil fell down the chimbly and crippled his back for life, everybody said it would be a lesson to him. What kind of a lesson? How was he going to use it? He could n't climb chimblies no more, and he had n't no more backs to break."

"All de same, Mars Tom, dey *is* sich a thing as learnin' by expe'ence. De Good Book say de burnt chile shun de fire."

"Well, I ain't denying that a thing 's a lesson if it 's a thing that can happen twice just the same way. There 's lots of such things, and *they* educate a person, that 's what uncle Abner always said; but there 's forty *million* lots of the other kind—the kind that don't happen the same way twice—and they ain't no real use, they ain't no more instructive than the small pox. When

you 've got it, it ain't no good to find out you
ought to been vaccinated, and it ain't no good
to get vaccinated afterwards, because the small-
pox don't come but once. But on the other
hand uncle Abner said that the person that had
took a bull by the tail once had learnt sixty or
seventy times as much as a person that had n't,
and said a person that started in to carry a cat
home by the tail was gitting knowledge that was
always going to be useful to him, and war n't
ever going to grow dim or doubtful. But I can
tell you, Jim, uncle Abner was down on them
people that 's all the time trying to dig a lesson out of everything that happens, no matter
whether—"

But Jim was asleep. Tom looked kind of
ashamed, because you know a person always
feels bad when he is talking uncommon fine and
thinks the other person is admiring, and that
other person goes to sleep that way. Of course
he ought n't to go to sleep, because it 's shabby ;
but the finer a person talks the certainer it is to
make you sleep, and so when you come to look
at it it ain't nobody's fault in particular, both of
them 's to blame.

Jim begun to snore — soft and blubbery, at

first, then a long rasp, then a stronger one, then a half a dozen horrible ones like the last water sucking down the plug-hole of a bath-tub, then the same with more power to it, and some big coughs and snorts flung in, the way a cow does that is choking to death; and when the person has got to that point he is at his level best, and can wake up a man that is in the next block with a dipper full of loddanum in him, but can't wake himself up although all that awful noise of his'n ain't but three inches from his own ears. And that is the curiosest thing in the world, seems to me. But you rake a match to light the candle, and that little bit of a noise will fetch him. I wish I knowed what was the reason of that, but there don't seem to be no way to find out. Now there was Jim alarming the whole Desert, and yanking the animals out, for miles and miles around, to see what in the nation was going on up there; there war n't nobody nor nothing that was as close to the noise as *he* was, and yet he was the only cretur that was n't disturbed by it. We yelled at him and whooped at him, it never done no good, but the first time there come a little wee noise that was n't of a usual kind it woke him up. No, sir, I 've thought it all over, and so has Tom, and there ain't no way to find out why a snorer can't hear himself snore.

Jim said he had n't been asleep, he just shut his eyes so he could listen better.

Tom said nobody war n't accusing him.

That made him look like he wished he had n't said anything. And he wanted to git away from the subject, I reckon, because he begun to abuse the camel driver, just the way a person does when he has got catched in something and wants to take it out of somebody else. He let into the camel driver the hardest he knowed how, and I had to agree with him; and he praised up the dervish the highest he could, and I had to agree with him there, too. But Tom says—

"I ain't so sure. You call that dervish so dreadful liberal and good and unselfish, but I don't quite see it. He did n't hunt up another poor dervish, did he? No, he did n't. If he was so unselfish, why did n't he go in there himself and take a pocket full of jewels and go along and be satisfied? No, sir, the person he was hunting for was a man with a hundred camels. He wanted to get away with all the treasure he could."

"Why, Mars Tom, he was willin' to divide, fair and square ; he only struck for fifty camels."

" Because he knowed how he was going to get all of them by and by."

" Mars Tom, he *tole* de man de truck would make him bline."

" Yes, because he knowed the man's character. It was just the kind of a man he was hunting for —a man that never believes in anybody's word or anybody's honorableness, because he ain't got none of his own. I reckon there 's lots of people like that dervish. They swindle, right and left, but they always make the other person *seem* to swindle himself. They keep inside of the letter of the law all the time, and there ain't no way to git hold of them. *They* don't put the salve on—oh, no, that would be sin ; but they know how to fool *you* into putting it on, then it 's you that blinds yourself. I reckon the dervish and the camel driver was just a pair—a fine, smart, brainy rascal, and a dull, coarse, ignorant one, but both of them rascals, just the same."

"Mars Tom, does you reckon dey 's any o' dat kind o' salve in de worl' now ? "

" Yes, uncle Abner says there is. He says they 've got it in New York, and they put it on country people's eyes and show them all the railroads in the world, and they go in and git them, and then when they rub the salve on the other eye the other man bids them good-by and goes off with their railroads. Here's the treasure-hill, now. Lower away!"

We landed, but it war n't as interesting as I thought it was going to be, because we could n't find the place where they went in to git the treasure. Still, it was plenty interesting enough, just to see the mere hill itself where such a wonderful thing happened. Jim said he would n't 'a' missed it for three dollars, and I felt the same way.

And to me and Jim, as wonderful a thing as any was the way Tom could come into a strange big country like this and go straight and find a little hump like that and tell it in a minute from a million other humps that was almost just like it, and nothing to help him but only his own learning and his own natural smartness. We talked and talked it over together, but could n't make out how he done it. He had the best head on him I ever see; and all he lacked was age, to make a name for himself equal to Captain Kidd or George Washington. I bet you it would 'a' crowded either of *them* to find that hill, with all their gifts, but it war n't nothing to Tom Sawyer; he went across Sahara and put his finger on it as easy as you could pick a nigger out of a bunch of angels.

We found a pond of salt water close by and scraped up a raft of salt around the edges and loaded up the lion's skin and the tiger's so as they would keep till Jim could tan them.

CHAPTER XI.

THE SAND-STORM.

WE went a-fooling along for a day or two, and then just as the full moon was touching the ground on the other side of the desert, we see a string of little black figgers moving across its big silver face. You could see them as plain as if they was painted on the moon with ink. It was another caravan. We cooled down our speed and tagged along after it, just to have company, though it war n't going our way. It was a rattler, that caravan, and a most bully sight to look at, next morning when the sun come a-streaming across the desert and flung the long shadders of the camels on the gold sand like a thousand grand-daddy-longlegses marching in procession. We never went very near it, because we knowed better, now, than to act like that and scare people's camels and break up their caravans. It was the gayest outfit you ever see, for rich clothes and nobby style. Some of the chiefs rode on dromedaries, the first we ever see, and very tall, and they go plunging along like they was on stilts, and they rock the man that is on them pretty violent and churn up his dinner considerable, I bet you, but they make noble good time and a camel ain't nowheres with them for speed.

The caravan camped, during the middle part of the day, and then started again about the middle of the afternoon. Before long the sun begun to look very curious. First it kind of turned to brass, and then to copper, and after that it begun to look like a blood-red ball, and the air got hot and close, and pretty soon all the sky in the west darkened up and looked thick and foggy, but fiery and dreadful like it looks through a piece of red glass, you know. We looked down and see a big confusion going on in the caravan and a rushing every which way like they was scared, and then they all flopped down flat in the sand and laid there perfectly still.

Pretty soon we see something coming that stood up like an amazing wide wall, and reached from the desert up into the sky and hid the sun, and it was coming like the nation, too. Then a little faint breeze struck us, and then it come harder, and grains of sand begun to sift against our faces and sting like fire, and Tom sung out—

" It 's a sand-storm—turn your backs to it!"

We done it, and in another minute it was blowing a gale and the sand beat against us by the shovelfull and the air was so thick with it we could n't see a thing. In five minutes the boat was level full and we was setting on the lockers buried up to the chin in sand and only our heads out and could hardly breathe.

Then the storm thinned, and we see that monstrous wall go a-sailing off across the desert, awful to look at, I tell you. We dug ourselves out and looked down, and where the caravan was before, there was n't anything but just the sand ocean, now, and all still and quiet. All them people and camels was smothered and dead and buried—buried under ten foot of sand, we reckoned, and Tom allowed it might be years before the wind uncovered them, and all that time their friends would n't ever know what become of that caravan. Tom said—

" *Now* we know what it was that happened to the people we got the swords and pistols from."

Yes, sir, that was just it. It was as plain as day, now. They got buried in a sand-storm, and the wild animals could n't get at them, and the wind never uncovered them again till they was

IN THE SAND-STORM.

dried to leather and war n't fit to eat. It seemed to me we had felt as sorry for them poor people as a person could for anybody, and as mournful, too, but we was mistaken; this last caravan's death went harder with us, a good deal harder. You see, the others was total strangers, and we never got to feeling acquainted with them at all, except, maybe, a little with the man that was watching the girl, but it was different with this last caravan. We was huvvering around them a whole night and 'most a whole day, and had got to feeling real friendly with them, and acquainted. I have found out that there ain't no surer way to find out whether you like people or hate them, than to travel with them. Just so with these. We kind of liked them from the start, and traveling with them put on the finisher. The longer we traveled with them, and the more we got used to their ways, the better and better we liked them and the gladder and gladder we was that we run across them. We had come to know some of them so well that we called them by name when we was talking about them, and soon got so familiar and sociable that we even dropped the Miss and the Mister and just used their plain names without any handle, and it did not seem unpolite, but just the right thing. Of course it was n't their own names, but names we give them. There was Mr. Elexander Robinson and Miss Adaline Robinson, and Col. Jacob McDougal, and Miss Harryet McDougal, and Judge Jeremiah Butler and young Bushrod Butler, and these was big chiefs, mostly, that wore splendid great turbans and simmeters, and dressed like the Grand Mogul, and their families. But as soon as we come to know them good, and like them very much, it war n't Mister, nor Judge, nor nothing, any more, but only Elleck, and Addy, and Jake, and Hattie, and Jerry and Buck, and so on.

And you know, the more you join in with people in their joys and their sorrows, the more nearer and dearer they come to be to you. Now we war n't cold and indifferent, the way most travelers is, we was right down friendly and sociable, and took a chance in everything that was going, and the caravan could depend on us to be on hand every time, it did n't make no difference what it was.

When they camped, we camped right over them, ten or twelve hundred feet up in the air. When they et a meal, we et ourn, and it made it ever so much homeliker to have their company.

When they had a wedding, that night, and Buck and Addy got married, we got ourselves up in the very starchiest of the professor's duds for the blow-out, and when they danced we jined in and shook a foot up there.

But it is sorrow and trouble that brings you the nearest, and it was a funeral that done it with us. It was next morning, just in the still dawn. We did n't know the diseased, and he war n't in our set, but that never made no difference, he belonged to the caravan, and that was enough, and there war n't no more sincerer tears shed over him than the ones we dripped on him from up there eleven hundred foot on high.

Yes, parting with this caravan was much more bitterer than it was to part with them others, which was comparative strangers, and been dead so long, anyway. We had knowed these in their lives, and was fond of them, too, and now to have death snatch them from right before our faces whilst we was looking, and leave us so lonesome and friendless in the middle of that big desert, it did hurt so, and we wished we might n't ever make any more friends on that voyage if we was going to lose them again like that.

We could n't keep from talking about them,

and they was all the time coming up in our memory, and looking just the way they looked when we was all alive and happy together. We could see the line marching, and the shiny spear-heads a-winking in the sun, we could see the dromedaries lumbering along, we could see the wedding and the funeral, and more oftener than anything else we could see them praying, be-cause they don't allow nothing to prevent that ; whenever the call come, several times a day, they would stop right there, and stand up and face to the east, and lift back their heads, and spread out their arms and begin, and four or five times they would go down on their knees, and then fall forwards and touch their forehead to the ground.

Well, it war n't good to go on talking about them, lovely as they was in their life, and dear to us in their life and death both, because it did n't do no good, and made us too down-hearted. Jim allowed he was going to live as good a life as he could, so he could see them again in a better world ; and Tom kept still and did n't tell him they was only Mohammedans, it war n't no use to disappoint him, he was feeling bad enough just as it was.

THE WEDDING PROCESSION.

When we woke up next morning we was feeling a little cheerfuller, and had had a most powerful good sleep, because sand is the comfort-
ablest bed there is, and I don't see why people
that can afford it don't have it more. And it 's
terrible good ballast, too ; I never see the balloon
so steady before.

Tom allowed we had twenty tons of it, and
wondered what we better do with it ; it was good
sand, and it did n't seem good sense to throw it
away. Jim says—

" Mars Tom, can't we tote it back home en sell
it ? How long 'll it take ? "

" Depends on the way we go."

" Well, sah, she 's wuth a quarter of a dollar a
load, at home, en I reckon we 's got as much as
twenty loads, hain't we ? How much would dat
be ? "

" Five dollars."

" By jings, Mars Tom, le's shove for home
right on de spot ! Hit 's more 'n a dollar en a
half apiece, hain't it ? "

" Yes."

" Well, ef dat ain't makin' money de easiest
ever *I* struck ! She jes' rained in—never cos' us a
lick o' work. Le's mosey right along, Mars Tom."

But Tom was thinking and ciphering away so busy and excited he never heard him. Pretty soon he says—

"Five dollars—sho! Look here, this sand 's worth — worth — why, it 's worth no end of money."

"How is dat, Mars Tom? Go on, honey, go on!"

"Well, the minute people knows it 's genuwyne sand from the genuwyne Desert of Sahara, they 'll just be in a perfect state of mind to git hold of some of it to keep on the what-not in a vial with a label on it for a curiosity. All we got to do, is, to put it up in vials and float around all over the United States and peddle them out at ten cents apiece. We 've got all of ten thousand dollars' worth of sand in this boat."

Me and Jim went all to pieces with joy, and begun to shout whoopjamboreehoo, and Tom says—

"And we can keep on coming back and fetching sand, and coming back and fetching more sand, and just keep it a-going till we 've carted this whole desert over there and sold it out; and there ain't ever going to be any opposition, either, because we 'll take out a patent."

"My goodness," I says, "we 'll be as rich as Creosote, won't we, Tom?"

" Yes—Creesus, you mean. Why, that dervish was hunting in that little hill for the treasures of the earth, and did n't know he was walking over the real ones for a thousand miles. He was blinder than he made the driver."

" Mars Tom, how much is we gwyne to be worth?"

" Well, I don't know, yet. It 's got to be ciphered, and it ain't the easiest job to do, either, because it 's over four million square miles of sand at ten cents a vial."

Jim was awful excited, but this faded it out considerable, and he shook his head and says—

" Mars Tom, we can't 'ford all dem vials—a king could n't. We better not try to take de whole desert, Mars Tom, de vials gwyne to bust us, sho'."

Tom's excitement died out, too, now, and I reckoned it was on account of the vials, but it was n't. He set there thinking, and got bluer and bluer, and at last he says—

" Boys, it won't work; we got to give it up."

" Why, Tom?"

" On account of the duties."

I could n't make nothing out of that, neither could Jim. I says—

"What *is* our duty, Tom? Because if we can't git around it, why can't we just *do* it? People often has to."

But he says—

"Oh, it ain't that kind of duty. The kind I mean is a tax. Whenever you strike a frontier—that's the border of a country, you know—you find a custom house there, and the gov'ment officers comes and rummages amongst your things and charges a big tax, which they call a duty because it's their duty to bust you if they can, and if you don't pay the duty they'll hog your sand. They call it confiscating, but that don't deceive nobody, it's just hogging, and that's all it is. Now if we try to carry this sand home the way we're pointed now, we got to climb fences till we git tired—just frontier after frontier—Egypt, Arabia, Hindostan, and so on, and they'll all whack on a duty, and so you see, easy enough, we *can't* go *that* road."

"Why, Tom," I says, "we can sail right over their old frontiers; how are *they* going to stop us?"

He looked sorrowful at me, and says, very grave—

"WHEN THEY DANCED WE JOINED IN AND SHOOK A FOOT UP THERE."

"Huck Finn, do you think that would be honest?"

I hate them kind of interruptions. I never said nothing, and he went on—

"Well, we 're shut off the other way, too. If we go back the way we 've come, there 's the New York custom house, and that is worse than all of them others put together, on account of the kind of cargo we 've got."

"Why?"

"Well, they can't raise Sahara sand in America, of course, and when they can't raise a thing there, the duty is fourteen hundred thousand per cent. on it if you try to fetch it in from where they do raise it."

"There ain't no sense in that, Tom Sawyer."

"Who said there *was*? What do you talk to me like that, for, Huck Finn? You wait till I say a thing 's got sense in it before you go to accusing me of saying it."

"All right, consider me crying about it, and sorry. Go on."

Jim says—

"Mars Tom, do dey jam dat duty onto everything we can't raise in America, en don't make no 'stinction 'twix' anything?"

" Yes, that 's what they do."

" Mars Tom, ain't de blessin' o' de Lord de mos' valuable thing dey is?"

" Yes, it is."

" Don't de preacher stan' up in de pulpit en call it down on de people?"

" Yes."

" Whah do it come from?"

" From heaven."

" Yassir! you 's jes' right, 'deed you is, honey —it come from heaven, en dat 's a foreign country. *Now* den! de dey put a tax on dat blessin'?"

" No, they don't."

" 'Course dey don't; en so it stan' to reason dat you 's mistaken, Mars Tom. Dey would n't put de tax on po' truck like san', dat everybody ain't 'bleeged to have, en leave it off'n de bes' thing dey is, which nobody can't git along widout."

Tom Sawyer was stumped; he see Jim had got him where he could n't budge. He tried to wiggle out by saying they had *forgot* to put on that tax, but they 'd be sure to remember about it, next session of Congress, and then they 'd put it on, but that was a poor lame come-off, and he

knowed it. He said there war n't nothing foreign that war n't taxed but just that one, ar d so
they could n't be consistent without taxing it,
and to be consistent was the first law of politics.
So he stuck to it that they 'd left it out unin-
tentional and would be certain to do their best to
fix it before they got caught and laughed at.

But I did n't feel no more interest in such
things, as long as we could n't git our sand
through, and it made me low-spirited, and Jim
the same. Tom he tried to cheer us up by saying he would think up another speculation for us
that would be just as good as this one and better, but it did n't do no good, we did n't believe
there was any as big as this. It was mighty
hard ; such a little while ago we was so rich, and
could 'a' bought a country and started a kingdom
and been celebrated and happy, and now we
was so poor and ornery again, and had our sand
left on our hands. The sand was looking so
lovely, before, just like gold and dimonds, and
the feel of it was so soft and so silky and nice,
but now I could n't bear the sight of it, it made
me sick to look at it, and I knowed I would n't
ever feel comfortable again till we got shut of it,
and I did n't have it there no more to remind us

of what we had been and what we had de-
graded down to. The others was feeling the
same way about it that I was. I knowed it, because they cheered up so, the minute I says le' 's
throw this truck overboard.

Well, it was going to be work, you know, and
pretty solid work, too ; so Tom he divided it up
according to fairness and strength. He said me
and him would clear out a fifth apiece, of the
sand, and Jim three fifths. Jim he did n't quite
like that arrangement, He says—

" 'Course I 's de stronges', en I 's willin' to do
a share accordin', but by jings you 's kinder
pilin' it onto ole Jim, Mars Tom, hain't you ? "

"Well, I did n't think so, Jim, but you try
your hand at fixing it, and let 's see."

So Jim he reckoned it would n't be no more
than fair if me and Tom done a *tenth* apiece.
Tom he turned his back to git room and be private, and then he smole a smile that spread
around and covered the whole Sahara to the
westward, back to the Atlantic edge of it where
we come from. Then he turned around again
and said it was a good enough arrangement, and
we was satisfied if Jim was. Jim said he was.

So then Tom measured off our two tenths in

the bow and left the rest for Jim, and it surprised Jim a good deal to see how much difference there was and what a raging lot of sand his share come to, and said he was powerful glad, now, that he had spoke up in time and got the first arrangement altered, for he said that even the way it was now, there was more sand than enjoyment in his end of the contract, he believed.

Then we laid into it. It was mighty hot work, and tough ; so hot we had to move up into cooler weather or we could n't 'a' stood it. Me and Tom took turn about, and one worked while t' other rested, but there war n't nobody to spell poor old Jim, and he made all that part of Africa damp, he sweated so. We could n't work good, we was so full of laugh, and Jim he kept fretting and wanting to know what tickled us so, and we had to keep making up things to account for it, and they was pretty poor inventions, but they done well enough, Jim did n't see through them. At last when we got done we was 'most dead, but not with work but with laughing. By and by Jim was 'most dead too, but it was with work ; then we took turns and spelled him, and he was as thankful as he could be, and would set on the gunnel and swab the sweat, and heave and pant, and say how good we was to a poor old nigger, and he would n't ever forgit us. He was always the gratefulest nigger I ever see, for any little thing you done for him. He was only nigger outside; inside he was as white as you be.

CHAPTER XII.

THE next few meals was pretty sandy, but that don't make no difference when you are hungry; and when you ain't it ain't no satisfaction to eat, anyway, and so a little grit in the meat ain't no particular drawback, as far as I can see.

Then we struck the east end of the desert at last, sailing on a north-east course. Away off on the edge of the sand, in a soft pinky light, we see three little sharp roofs like tents, and Tom says—

"It's the pyramids of Egypt."

It made my heart fairly jump. You see, I had seen a many and a many a picture of them, and heard tell about them a hundred times, and yet to come on them all of a sudden, that way, and find they was *real*, 'stead of imaginations 'most knocked the breath out of me with surprise. It's a curious thing, that the more you hear about a grand and big and bully thing or person, the more it kind of dreamies out, as you

183

may say, and gets to be a big dim wavery figger
made out of moonshine and nothing solid to it.
It 's just so with George Washington, and the
same with them pyramids.

And moreover besides, the thing they always
said about them seemed to me to be stretchers.
There was a feller come to the Sunday-school,
once, and had a picture of them, and made a
speech, and said the biggest pyramid covered
thirteen acres, and was most five hundred foot
high, just a steep mountain, all built out of
hunks of stone as big as a bureau, and laid up
in perfectly regular layers, like stair-steps.
Thirteen acres, you see, for just one building:
it 's a farm.   If it had n't been in Sunday-school,
I would 'a' judged it was a lie ; and outside I was
certain of it.   And he said there was a hole in
the pyramid, and you could go in there with
candles, and go ever so far up a long slanting
tunnel, and come to a large room in the stomach
of that stone mountain, and there you would
find a big stone chest with a king in it, four
thousand years old.   I said to myself, then, if
that ain't a lie I will eat that king if they will
fetch him, for even Methusalem war n't that old,
and nobody claims it.

As we come a little nearer we see the yaller sand come to an end in a long straight edge like a blanket, and onto it was joined, edge to edge, a wide country of bright green, with a snaky stripe crooking through it, and Tom said it was the Nile. It made my heart jump again, for the Nile was another thing that was n't real to me. Now I can tell you one thing which is dead certain: if you will fool along over three thousand miles of yaller sand, all glimmering with heat so that it makes your eyes water to look at it, and you 've been a considerable part of a week doing it, the green country will look so like home and heaven to you that it will make your eyes water *again*.

It was just so with me, and the same with Jim.

And when Jim got so he could believe it *was* the land of Egypt he was looking at, he would n't enter it standing up, but got down on his knees and took off his hat, because he said it was n't fitten' for a humble poor nigger to come any other way where such men had been as Moses and Joseph and Pharaoh and the other prophets. He was a Presbyterian, and had a most deep respect for Moses which was a Presbyterian too, he said. He was all stirred up, and says—

"Hit 's de lan' of Egypt, de lan' of Egypt, en I 's 'lowed to look at it wid my own eyes! En dah 's de river dat was turn' to blood, en I 's looking at de very same groun' whah de plagues was, en de lice, en de frogs, en de locus', en de hail, en whah dey marked de door-pos', en de angel o' de Lord come by in de darkness o' de night en slew de fust-born in all de lan' o' Egypt. Ole Jim ain't worthy to see dis day!"

And then he just broke down and cried, he was so thankful. So between him and Tom there was talk enough, Jim being excited because the land was so full of history — Joseph and his brethren, Moses in the bulrushers, Jacob coming down into Egypt to buy corn, the silver cup in the sack, and all them interesting things, and Tom just as excited too, because the land was so full of history that was in *his* line, about Noureddin, and Bedreddin, and such like monstrous giants, that made Jim's wool rise, and a raft of other Arabian Nights folks, which the half of them never done the things they let on they done, I don't believe.

Then we struck a disappointment, for one of

them early - morning fogs started up, and it
war n't no use to sail over the top of it, because
we would go by Egypt, sure, so we judged it
was best to set her by compass straight for the
place where the pyramids was gitting blurred
and blotted out, and then drop low and skin
along pretty close to the ground and keep a
sharp lookout. Tom took the hellum, I stood
by to let go the anchor, and Jim he straddled
the bow to dig through the fog with his eyes
and watch out for danger ahead. We went
along a steady gait, but not very fast, and the
fog got solider and solider, so solid that Jim
looked dim and ragged and smoky through it.
It was awful still, and we talked low and was
anxious. Now and then Jim would say—

"Highst her a p'int, Mars Tom, highst her!"
and up she would skip, a foot or two, and we
would slide right over a flat-roofed mud cabin,
with people that had been asleep on it just be-
ginning to turn out and gap and stretch; and
once when a feller was clear up on his hind legs
so he could gap and stretch better, we took him
a blip in the back and knocked him off. By and
by, after about an hour, and everything dead
still and we a-straining our ears for sounds and

holding our breath, the fog thinned a little, very sudden, and Jim sung out in an awful scare—

"Oh, for de lan's sake, set her back, Mars Tom, here's de biggest giant outen de 'Rabian Nights a-comin' for us!" and he went over backwards in the boat.

Tom slammed on the back-action, and as we slowed to a standstill, a man's face as big as our house at home looked in over the gunnel, same as a house looks out of its windows, and I laid down and died. I must 'a' been clear dead and gone for as much as a minute or more; then I come to, and Tom had hitched a boat-hook onto the lower lip of the giant and was holding the balloon steady with it whilst he canted his head back and got a good long look up at that awful face.

Jim was on his knees with his hands clasped, gazing up at the thing in a begging way, and working his lips but not getting anything out. I took only just a glimpse, and was fading out again, but Tom says—

"He ain't alive, you fools, it's the Sphinx!"

I never see Tom look so little and like a fly; but that was because the giant's head was so big and awful. Awful, yes, so it was, but not dread-

ful, any more, because you could see it was a
noble face, and kind of sad, and not thinking
about you, but about other things and larger.
It was stone, reddish stone, and its nose and
ears battered, and that give it an abused look,
and you felt sorrier for it, for that.

We stood off a piece, and sailed around it and
over it, and it was just grand. It was a man's
head, or maybe a woman's, on a tiger's body a
hundred and twenty-five foot long, and there
was a dear little temple between its front paws.
All but the head used to be under the sand, for
hundreds of years, maybe thousands, but they
had just lately dug the sand away and found
that little temple. It took a power of sand to
bury that cretur; most as much as it would to
bury a steamboat, I reckon.

We landed Jim on top of the head, with an
American flag to protect him, it being a foreign
land, then we sailed off to this and that and
t' other distance, to git what Tom called effects
and perspectives and proportions, and Jim he
done the best he could, striking all the different
kinds of attitudes and positions he could study
up, but standing on his head and working his
legs the way a frog does was the best. The

further we got away, the littler Jim got, and the
grander the Sphinx got, till at last it was only a
clothes-pin on a dome, as you might say.
That 's the way perspective brings out the correct proportions, Tom said ; he said Julus Cesar's
niggers did n't know how big he was, they was
too close to him.

Then we sailed off further and further, till we
could n't see Jim at all, any more, and then that
great figger was at its noblest, a-gazing out over
the Nile valley so still and solemn and lonesome,
and all the little shabby huts and things that
was scattered about it clean disappeared and
gone, and nothing around it now but a soft wide
spread of yaller velvet, which was the sand.

That was the right place to stop, and we done
it. We set there a-looking and a-thinking for a
half an hour, nobody a-saying anything, for it
made us feel quiet and kind of solemn to remember it had been looking over that valley just that
same way, and thinking its awful thoughts all
to itself for thousands of years, and nobody
can't find out what they are to this day.

At last I took up the glass and see some little
black things a-capering around on that velvet
carpet, and some more a-climbing up the cretur's

JIM STANDING A SIEGE.

back, and then I see two or three wee puffs of
white smoke, and told Tom to look. He done
it, and says—

"They 're bugs. No—hold on ; they—why, I
believe they 're men. Yes, it 's men—men and
horses, both. They 're hauling a long ladder up
onto the Sphinx's back — now ain't that odd ?
And now they 're trying to lean it up a—there 's
some more puffs of smoke—it 's guns! Huck,
they 're after Jim!"

We clapped on the power, and went for them
a-biling. We was there in no time, and come
a-whizzing down amongst them, and they broke
and scattered every which way, and some that
was climbing the ladder after Jim let go all holts
and fell. We soared up and found him laying
on top of the head panting and most tuckered
out, partly from howling for help and partly
from scare. He had been standing a siege a
long time—a week, *he* said, but it war n't so, it
only just seemed so to him because they was
crowding him so. They had shot at him, and
rained the bullets all around him, but he war n't
hit, and when they found he would n't stand up
and the bullets could n't git at him when he was
laying down, they went for the ladder, and then

he knowed it was all up with him if we did n't
come pretty quick. Tom was very indignant,
and asked him why he did n't show the flag and
command them to *git*, in the name of the United
States. Jim said he done it, but they never paid
no attention. Tom said he would have this
thing looked into at Washington, and says—

"You 'll see that they 'll have to apologize for
insulting the flag, and pay an indemnity, too, on
top of it, even if they git off *that* easy."

Jim says—

"What 's an indemnity, Mars Tom?"

"It 's cash, that 's what it is."

"Who gits it, Mars Tom?"

"Why, *we* do."

"En who gits de apology?"

"The United States. Or, we can take whichever we please. We can take the apology, if we
want to, and let the gov'ment take the money."

"How much money will it be, Mars Tom?"

"Well, in an aggravated case like this one, it
will be at least three dollars apiece, and I don't
know but more."

"Well, den, we 'll take de money, Mars Tom,
blame de 'pology. Hain't dat yo' notion, too?
En hain't it yourn, Huck?"

We talked it over a little and allowed that that
was as good a way as any, so we agreed to take
the money. It was a new business to me, and I
asked Tom if countries always apologized when
they had done wrong, and he says—

" Yes ; the little ones does."

We was sailing around examining the pyramids, you know, and now we soared up and
roosted on the flat top of the biggest one, and
found it was just like what the man said in the
Sunday-school. It was like four pairs of stairs
that starts broad at the bottom and slants up
and comes together in a point at the top, only
these stair-steps could n't be clumb the way you
climb other stairs ; no, for each step was as high
as your chin, and you have to be boosted up from
behind. The two other pyramids war n't far
away, and the people moving about on the sand
between looked like bugs crawling, we was so
high above them.

Tom he could n't hold himself he was so
worked up with gladness and astonishment to
be in such a celebrated place, and he just dripped
history from every pore, seemed to me. He said
he could n't scarcely believe he was standing on
the very identical spot the prince flew from on

the Bronze Horse. It was in the Arabian Night
times, he said. Somebody give the prince a
bronze horse with a peg in its shoulder, and he
could git on him and fly through the air like a
bird, and go all over the world, and steer it by
turning the peg, and fly high or low and land
wherever he wanted to.

When he got done telling it there was one of
them uncomfortable silences that comes, you
know, when a person has been telling a whopper
and you feel sorry for him and wish you could
think of some way to change the subject and let
him down easy, but git stuck and don't see no
way, and before you can pull your mind together
and *do* something, that silence has got in and
spread itself and done the business. I was embarrassed, Jim he was embarrassed, and neither
of us could n't say a word. Well, Tom he glow-
ered at me a minute, and says—

"Come, out with it. What do you think?"

I says—

"Tom Sawyer, *you* don't believe that, yourself."

"What 's the reason I don't? What 's to hender
me?"

"There 's one thing to hender you : it could n't
happen, that 's all."

" What 's the reason it could n't happen ? "

" You tell me the reason it *could* happen."

" This balloon is a good enough reason it could happen, I should reckon."

" *Why* is it ? "

" *Why* is it ? I never saw such an idiot. Ain't this balloon and the bronze horse the same thing under different names ? "

" No, they 're not. One is a balloon and the other 's a horse. It 's very different. Next you 'll be saying a house and a cow is the same thing."

" By Jackson, Huck 's got him ag'in ! Dey ain't no wigglin' outer dat ! "

" Shut your head, Jim ; you don't know what you 're talking about. And Huck don't. Look here, Huck, I 'll make it plain to you, so you can understand. You see, it ain't the mere *form* that's got anything to do with their being similar or unsimilar, it 's the *principle* involved ; and the principle is the same in both. Don't you see, now ? "

I turned it over in my mind, and says—

" Tom, it ain't no use. Principles is all very well, but they don't git around that one big fact, that the thing that a balloon can do ain't no sort of proof of what a horse can do."

"Shucks, Huck, you don't get the idea at all. Now look here a minute—it's perfectly plain. Don't we fly through the air?"

"Yes."

"Very well. Don't we fly high or fly low, just as we please?"

"Yes."

"Don't we steer whichever way we want to?"

"Yes."

"And don't we land when and where we please?"

"Yes."

"How do we move the balloon and steer it?"

"By touching the buttons."

"*Now* I reckon the thing is clear to you at last. In the other case the moving and steering was done by turning a peg. We touch a button, the prince turned a peg. There ain't an atom of difference, you see. I knowed I could git it through your head if I stuck to it long enough."

He felt so happy he begun to whistle. But me and Jim was silent, so he broke off surprised, and says—

"Looky here, Huck Finn, don't you see it *yet?*"

I says—

RESCUE OF JIM.

"Tom Sawyer, I want to ask you some questions."

"Go ahead," he says, and I see Jim chirk up to listen.

"As I understand it, the whole thing is in the buttons and the peg—the rest ain't of no consequence. A button is one shape, a peg is another shape, but that ain't any matter?"

"No, that ain't any matter, as long as they 've both got the same power."

"All right, then. What is the power that 's in a candle and in a match?"

"It 's the fire."

"It 's the same in both, then?"

"Yes, just the same in both."

"All right. Suppose I set fire to a carpenter shop with a match, what will happen to that carpenter shop?"

"She 'll burn up."

"And suppose I set fire to this pyramid with a candle—will she burn up?"

"Of course she won't."

"All right. Now the fire 's the same, both times. *Why* does the shop burn, and the pyramid don't?"

"Because the pyramid *can't* burn."

"Aha! and *a horse can't fly!*"

"My lan', ef Huck ain't got him ag'in! Huck 's landed him high en dry dis time, *I* tell you! Hit 's de smartes' trap I ever see a body walk inter—en ef I—"

But Jim was so full of laugh he got to strangling and could n't go on, and Tom was that mad to see how neat I had floored him, and turned his own argument ag'in him and knocked him all to rags and flinders with it that all he could manage to say was that whenever he heard me and Jim try to argue it made him ashamed of the human race. I never said nothing, I was feeling pretty well satisfied. When I have got the best of a person that way, it ain't my way to go around crowing about it the way some people does, for I consider that if I was in his place I would n't wish him to crow over me. It 's better to be generous, that 's what I think.

CHAPTER XIII.

GOING FOR TOM'S PIPE.

By and by we left Jim to float around up there in the neighborhood of the pyramids, and we clumb down to the hole where you go into the tunnel, and went in with some Arabs and candles, and away in there in the middle of the pyramid we found a room and a big stone box in it where they used to keep that king, just as the man in the Sunday-school said, but he was gone, now, somebody had got him. But I did n't take no interest in the place, because there could be ghosts there, of course; not fresh ones, but I don't like no kind.

So then we come out and got some little donkeys and rode a piece, and then went in a boat another piece, and then more donkeys, and got to Cairo; and all the way the road was as smooth and beautiful a road as ever I see, and had tall date pams on both sides, and naked children everywhere, and the men was as red as copper, and fine and strong and handsome. And

the city was a curiosity.   Such narrow streets—
why, they were just lanes, and crowded with people with turbans, and women with veils, and
everybody rigged out in blazing bright clothes and
all sorts of colors, and you wondered how the camels and the people got by each other in such narrow little cracks, but they done it—a perfect jam,
you see, and everybody noisy.   The stores war n't
big enough to turn around in, but you did n't
have to go in ; the storekeeper sat tailor fashion
on his counter, smoking his snaky long pipe, and
had his things where he could reach them to sell,
and he was just as good as in the street, for the
camel-loads brushed him as they went by.

Now and then a grand person flew by in a car-
riage with fancy dressed men running and yelling in front of it and whacking anybody with a
long rod that did n't get out of the way.   And
by and by along comes the Sultan riding horseback at the head of a procession, and fairly took
your breath away his clothes was so splendid ;
and everybody fell flat and laid on his stomach
while he went by.   I forgot, but a feller helped
me remember.   He was one that had a rod and
run in front.

There was churches, but they don't know

enough to keep Sunday, they keep Friday and
break the Sabbath. You have to take off your
shoes when you go in. There was crowds of men
and boys in the church, setting in groups on the
stone floor and making no end of noise—getting
their lessons by heart, Tom said, out of the Ko-
ran, which they think is a Bible, and people that
knows better knows enough to not let on. I
never see such a big church in my life before, and
most awful high, it was; it made you dizzy to
look up; our village church at home ain't a cir-
cumstance to it; if you was to put it in there,
people would think it was a dry-goods box.

What I wanted to see was a dervish, because I
was interested in dervishes on accounts of the one
that played the trick on the camel driver. So we
found a lot in a kind of a church, and they called
themselves Whirling Dervishes; and they did
whirl, too, I never see anything like it. They
had tall sugar-loaf hats on, and linen petticoats;
and they spun and spun and spun, round and
round like tops, and the petticoats stood out on
a slant, and it was the prettiest thing I ever see,
and made me drunk to look at it. They was all
Moslems, Tom said, and when I asked him what
a Moslem was, he said it was a person that was n't

a Presbyterian. So there is plenty of them in Missouri, though I did n't know it before.

We did n't see half there was to see in Cairo, because Tom was in such a sweat to hunt out places that was celebrated in history. We had a most tiresome time to find the granary where Joseph stored up the grain before the famine, and when we found it it war n't worth much to look at, being such an old tumble-down wreck, but Tom was satisfied, and made more fuss over it than I would make if I stuck a nail in my foot. How he ever found that place was too many for me. We passed as much as forty just like it before we came to it, and any of them would 'a' done for me, but none but just the right one would suit him ; I never see anybody so particular as Tom Sawyer. The minute he struck the right one he reconnized it as easy as I would reconnize my other shirt if I had one, but how he done it he could n't any more tell than he could fly ; he said so himself.

Then we hunted a long time for the house where the boy lived that learned the cadi how to try the case of the old olives and the new ones, and said it was out of the Arabian Nights and he would tell me and Jim about it when he got

time. Well, we hunted and hunted till I was
ready to drop, and I wanted Tom to give it up
and come next day and git somebody that knowed
the town and could talk Missourian and could
go straight to the place ; but no, he wanted to
find it himself, and nothing else would answer.
So on we went. Then at last the remarkablest
thing happened I ever see. The house was gone
—gone hundreds of years ago—every last rag of
it gone but just one mud brick. Now a person
would n't ever believe that a backwoods Missouri boy that had n't ever been in that town before could go and hunt that place over and find
that brick, but Tom Sawyer done it. I know he
done it, because I see him do it. I was right by
his very side at the time, and see him see the
brick and see him reconnize it. Well, I says to
myself, how *does* he do it ? is it knowledge, or
is it instink ?

Now there 's the facts, just as they happened :
let everybody explain it their own way. I 've
ciphered over it a good deal, and it 's my opinion that some of it is knowledge but the main
bulk of it is instink. The reason is this. Tom
put the brick in his pocket to give to a museum
with his name on it and the facts when he went

home, and I slipped it out and put another brick considerable like it in its place, and he did n't know the difference—but there was a difference, you see. I think that settles it—it 's mostly instink, not knowledge. Instink tells him where the exact *place* is for the brick to be in, and so he reconnizes it by the place it 's in, not by the look of the brick. If it was knowledge, not instink, he would know the brick again by the look of it the next time he seen it—which he did n't. So it shows that for all the brag you hear about knowledge being such a wonderful thing, instink is worth forty of it for real unerringness. Jim says the same.

When we got back Jim dropped down and took us in, and there was a young man there with a red skull cap and tassel on and a beautiful blue silk jacket and baggy trousers with a shawl around his waist and pistols in it that could talk English and wanted to hire to us as guide and take us to Mecca and Medina and Central Africa and everywheres for a half a dollar a day and his keep, and we hired him and left, and piled on the power, and by the time we was through dinner we was over the place where the Israelites crossed the Red Sea when Pharaoh tried to over-

HOMEWARD BOUND.

take them and was caught by the waters. We stopped, then, and had a good look at the place, and it done Jim good to see it. He said he could see it all, now, just the way it happened; he could see the Israelites walking along between the walls of water, and the Egyptians coming, from away off yonder, hurrying all they could, and see them start in as the Israelites went out, and then, when they was all in, see the walls tumble together and drown the last man of them. Then we piled on the power again and rushed away and huvvered over Mount Sinai, and saw the place where Moses broke the tables of stone, and where the children of Israel camped in the plain and worshipped the golden calf, and it was all just as interesting as could be, and the guide knowed every place as well as I know the village at home.

But we had an accident, now, and it fetched all the plans to a standstill. Tom's old ornery corn-cob pipe had got so old and swelled and warped that she could n't hold together any longer, notwithstanding the strings and bandages, but caved in and went to pieces. Tom he did n't know *what* to do. The professor's pipe would n't answer, it war n't anything but a mer-

shum, and a person that 's got used to a cob pipe
knows it lays a long ways over all the other pipes
in this world, and you can't git him to smoke any
other.   He would n't take mine, I could n't per-
suade him.   So there he was.

He thought it over, and said we must scour
around and see if we could roust out one in
Egypt or Arabia or around in some of these
countries, but the guide said no, it war n't no
use, they did n't have them.   So Tom was pretty
glum for a little while, then he chirked up and
said he 'd got the idea and knowed what to do.
He says—

"I 've got another corn-cob pipe, and it 's a
prime one, too, and nearly new.   It 's laying on
the rafter that 's right over the kitchen stove at
home in the village.   Jim, you and the guide will
go and get it, and me and Huck will camp here
on Mount Sinai till you come back."

"But Mars Tom, we could n't ever find de village.   I could find de pipe, 'caze I knows de
kitchen, but my lan', *we* can't ever find de village, nur Sent Louis, nur none o' dem places.
We don't know de way, Mars Tom."

That was a fact, and it stumped Tom for a
minute.   Then he said—

" Looky here, it can be done, sure ; and I 'll tell you how. You set your compass and sail west as straight as a dart, till you find the United States. It ain't any trouble, because it 's the first land you 'll strike the other side of the Atlantic. If it 's daytime when you strike it, bulge right on, straight west from the upper part of the Florida coast, and in an hour and three quarters you 'll hit the mouth of the Mississippi—at the speed that I 'm going to send you. You 'll be so high up in the air that the earth will be curved considerable — sorter like a washbowl turned upside down—and you 'll see a raft of rivers crawling around every which way, long before you get there, and you can pick out the Mississippi without any trouble. Then you can follow the river north nearly, an hour and three quarters, till you see the Ohio come in; then you want to look sharp, because you 're getting near. Away up to your left you 'll see another thread coming in—that 's the Missouri and is a little above St. Louis. You 'll come down low, then, so as you can examine the villages as you spin along. You 'll pass about twenty-five in the next fifteen minutes, and you 'll recognize ours when you see it—and if you don't, you can yell down and ask."

"Ef it 's dat easy, Mars Tom, I reckon we kin
do it—yassir, I knows we kin."

The guide was sure of it, too, and thought
that he could learn to stand his watch in a little
while.

"Jim can learn you the whole thing in a half
an hour," Tom said. "This balloon 's as easy to
manage as a canoe."

Tom got out the chart and marked out the
course and measured it, and says—

"To go back west is the shortest way, you
see. It 's only about seven thousand miles. If
you went east, and so on around, it 's over twice
as far." Then he says to the guide, "I want
you both to watch the tell-tale all through the
watches, and whenever it don't mark three hundred miles an hour, you go higher or drop lower
till you find a storm-current that 's going your
way. There 's a hundred miles an hour in this
old thing without any wind to help. There 's
two hundred-mile gales to be found, any time
you want to hunt for them."

"We 'll hunt for them, sir."

"See that you do. Sometimes you may have
to go up a couple of miles, and it 'll be p'ison
cold, but most of the time you 'll find your storm

a good deal lower.   If you can only strike a cyclone—that 's the ticket for you !   You 'll see by the professor's books that they travel west in these latitudes ; and they travel low, too."

Then he ciphered on the time, and says—

"Seven thousand miles, three hundred miles an hour — you can make the trip in a day — twenty-four hours.   This is Thursday ; you 'll be back here Saturday afternoon.   Come, now, hustle out some blankets and food and books and things for me and Huck, and you can start right along.   There ain't no occasion to fool around— I want a smoke, and the quicker you fetch that pipe the better."

All hands jumped for the things, and in eight minutes our things was out and the balloon was ready for America.   So we shook hands good-bye, and Tom give his last orders :

"It 's 10 minutes to 2 p. m., now, Mount Sinai time.   In 24 hours you 'll be home, and it 'll be 6 to-morrow morning, village time.   When you strike the village, land a little back of the top of the hill, in the woods, out of sight ; then you rush down, Jim, and shove these letters in the post-office, and if you see anybody stirring, pull your slouch down over your face so they won't know

you. Then you go and slip in the back way, to
the kitchen and git the pipe, and lay this piece
of paper on the kitchen table and put something
on it to hold it, and then slide out and git away
and don't let Aunt Polly catch a sight of you,
nor nobody else. Then you jump for the balloon and shove for Mount Sinai three hundred
miles an hour. You won't have lost more than
an hour. You'll start back at 7 or 8 a. m., village
time, and be here in 24 hours, arriving at 2 or 3
p. m., Mount Sinai time."

Tom he read the piece of paper to us. He
had wrote on it—

"THURSDAY AFTERNOON. *Tom Sawyer the Erronort sends his love to Aunt Polly from Mount
Sinai where the Ark was, and so does Huck Finn,
and she will get it to-morrow morning half past
six.**

"TOM SAWYER THE ERRONORT."

"That 'll make her eyes bulge out and the
tears come," he says. Then he says—
"Stand by! One — two — three — away you
go!"

* This misplacing of the Ark is probably Huck's error, not Tom's.
                                                         —M. T.

And away she *did* go! Why, she seemed to whiz out of sight in a second.

Then we found a most comfortable cave that looked out over that whole big plain, and there we camped to wait for the pipe.

———

The balloon come back all right, and brung the pipe; but Aunt Polly had catched Jim when he was getting it, and anybody can guess what happened: she sent for Tom. So Jim he says—

"Mars Tom, she's out on de porch wid her eye sot on de sky a-layin' for you, en she say she ain't gwyne to budge from dah tell she gits hold of you. Dey's gwyne to be trouble, Mars Tom, 'deed dey is."

So then we shoved for home, and not feeling very gay, neither.

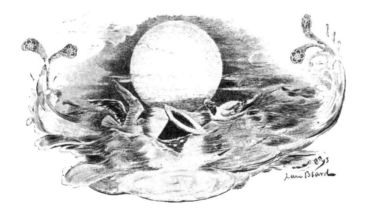

Popular New Books

FROM THE LIST OF

CHARLES L. WEBSTER & CO.

Mark Twain's Books.

Tom Sawyer Abroad.—By Huck Finn. Edited by Mark Twain. Stamped cloth, square octavo, 240 pages, with 28 illustrations from original drawings by Dan Beard. Price $1.50.

Adventures of Huckleberry Finn.—Holiday edition. Square 8vo, 368 pages. Illustrated by E. W. Kemble. Cloth, $2.75; sheep, $3.25.

New Cheap Edition of Huckleberry Finn.—12mo, 318 pages, with a few illustrations. Cloth, $1.00.

The Prince and the Pauper.—A square 8vo volume of 411 pages. Beautifully illustrated. Cloth, $3.00; sheep, $3.75.

New Cheap Edition of the Prince and the Pauper.—12mo, 300 pages, with illustrations. Cloth, $1.00.

A Connecticut Yankee in King Arthur's Court.—A square 8vo of 575 pages; 221 illustrations by Dan Beard. Cloth, $3.00; sheep, $4.00; half morocco, $5.00.

Mark Twain Holiday Set.—Three volumes in a box, consisting of the best editions of "Huckleberry Finn," "Prince and Pauper," and "A Connecticut Yankee." Square 8vo. Uniform in size, binding, and color. Sold only in sets. Cloth, $6.00.

Eighteen Short Stories and Sketches.—By Mark Twain. Including "The Stolen White Elephant," "Some Rambling Notes," "The Carnival of Crime," "A Curious Experience," "Punch, Brothers, Punch," "The Invalid's Story," etc., etc. 16mo, 306 pages. Cloth, $1.00.

Mark Twain's "Library of Humor."—A volume of 145 characteristic selections from the best writers, together with a short biographical sketch of each author quoted. Compiled by Mark Twain. Nearly 200 illustrations by E. W. Kemble. 8vo, 707 pages. Cloth, $3.50; sheep, $4.00; half seal, $4.25; half morocco, $5.00; full Turkey morocco, $7.00.

Life on the Mississippi.—8vo, 624 pages, and over 300 illustrations. Cloth, $3.50; sheep, $4.25.

Merry Tales.—In "Fiction, Fact, and Fancy Series." 12mo, 210 pages. Portrait frontispiece. This volume contains some of Mark Twain's most entertaining sketches. Among them are his personal reminiscences of the war in the "Private History of a Cmpaign that Failed," a short story entitled "Luck," and his popular farce "Meisterschaft." Cloth, gilt title, 75 cents.

The American Claimant.—8vo, 300 pages, fully illustrated by Dan Beard. The strong point in this story is that in it Mark Twain reintroduces to American readers his most famous character, Col. Mulberry Sellers. Cloth, $1.50.

The £1,000,000 Bank Note and Other Stories.—Small 8vo, 260 pages, with frontispiece by Dan Beard. The book contains other stories, many of which have never before appeared in print, and none in book form. Cloth, $1.00; leather, $1.50.

Miscellaneous.

Joanna Traill, Spinster.—By ANNIE E. HOLDSWORTH. Cloth, with special cover design, 12mo, 210 pages. Miss Holdsworth is one of the most popular of the younger English novelists, and in "Joanna Traill, Spinster" she has treated the now widely agitated question of individual rescue work among fallen women with great power, and at the same time with delicacy. The book presents a possible solution of the question, but is primarily a well-planned and interesting novel. Cloth, $1.25.

Alfred Lord Tennyson: A Study of His Life and Work.— By ARTHUR WAUGH, B. A. OXON. Illustrated, 350 pages. Mr. Arthur Waugh's "Alfred Lord Tennyson: A Study of His Life and Work," which was in process of revision at the time of the poet's death, and which was published soon after that event, has received such high praise from the critical press, that a description of its merits seems unnecessary. We beg to announce that we have arranged for the American publication of a new cheap edition of this work at half the former price, well printed, and with all the original illustrations, together with additions and revisions in the text. This standard working biography of the laureate is likely to retain its popularity among lovers of his verse. Cloth, $1.50.

On Sunny Shores.—By CLINTON SCOLLARD, author of "Under Summer Skies." 12mo, 300 pages. Illustrated by Margaret Landers Randolph. Professor Clinton Scollard has issued a further description of his poetical pilgrimages, entitled "On Sunny Shores." It is published as a companion volume to the popular "Under Summer Skies," the two works complementing each other. The charm of style and daintiness of touch shown in the former book travels is more than maintained. Cloth, $1.00.

Under Summer Skies.—Companion volume to the above. By CLINTON SCOLLARD. Illustrated by Margaret Landers Randolph. 12mo, 300 pages. A poet's itinerary. Professor Scollard relates, in his charming literary style, the episodes of a rambling tour through Egypt, Palestine, Italy, and the Alps. The text is interspersed with poetical interludes, suggested by passing events and scenes. Coming nearer home, visits to Arizona and the Bermudas are described in separate chapters. The volume is most suitable as a traveling companion or as a picture of lands beyond the reach of the reader. Cloth, $1.00.

The price of the two books in a box is $2.00.

Toppleton's Client; or, A Spirit in Exile.—JOHN KENDRICK BANGS. 12mo, 270 pages. A semi-humorous story of the supernatural in the best vein of this popular writer. An utterly commonplace English barrister is persuaded to vacate his body at intervals in favor of an accomplished but wicked disembodied soul. The latter achieves brilliant successes under its false guise, and finally makes off with the body altogether. The barrister's exiled spirit retains Toppleton to recover the lost body, and their efforts to do this are described in an entertaining manner. Cloth, $1.00.

In Beaver Cove and Elsewhere.—By MATT CRIM, author of "Adventures of a Fair Rebel." This volume contains all of Miss Crim's most famous short stories. These stories have received the highest praise from eminent critics, and have given Miss Crim a position among the leading lady writers of America. Illustrated by E. W. Kemble. Cloth, 8vo, $1.00. Paper, 50 cents.

Adventures of a Fair Rebel.—By MATT CRIM. This novel is the record of a deeply passionate nature, the interest in whose story is enhanced by her devotion to a lover, also a Southerner, compelled by his convictions to take service in the Northern army. Striking descriptions of the campaign in Georgia and the siege of Atlanta are given. With a frontispiece by Dan Beard. Cloth, 8vo, $1.00; paper, 50 cents.

Elizabeth : Christian Scientist. — By MATT CRIM. 12mo, 350 pages. The success of Miss Crim's previous works of fiction encourages us to announce her new novel with much confidence. The story deals with the career of a refined and deeply religious girl, who leaves her home in the Georgia mountains with the object of converting the world to Christian Science. Her romantic experiences in the great cities of the Union are vividly portrayed; and the fact that, after all, her destiny is to be loved and wedded does not detract from the book's interest. Cloth, $1.00; paper, 50 cents.

The Master of Silence. A Romance.—By IRVING BACHELLER. Readers of Mr. Bacheller's stories and poems in the magazines will look with interest for his first extended effort in fiction. ("Fiction, Fact, and Fancy Series.") Cloth, 12mo, 75 cents; paper 50 cents.

The Speech of Monkeys.—By R. L. GARNER. Mr. Garner's articles, published in the leading periodicals and journals touching upon this subject, have been widely read and favorably commented upon by scientific men both here and abroad. "The Speech of Monkeys" embodies his researches up to the present time. It is divided into two parts, the first being a record of experiments with monkeys and other animals, and the second part a treatise on the theory of speech. The work is written so as to bring the subject within reach of the casual reader without impairing its scientific value. Small 8vo, with Frontispiece, Cloth, $1.00.

The Art of Sketching.—By G. FRAIPONT. 12mo, 100 pages, with fifty illustrations from drawings by the author. Translated from the French by Clara Bell. With preface by Edwin Bale, R. I. That this little book is from the hand of a French artist will make it none the less acceptable to American students. Its references are mostly French because its author is so, and it is unnecessary, as well as undesirable, to disturb these in order to adapt them to American readers. The treatise is mainly intended for the use of artists in Black and White. It is short, but it is practical and good, and if Americans do not know the work of the French artists referred to, it will be a useful experience for them to search it out. Cloth, $1.00.

A Catastrophe in Bohemia.—By HENRY S. BROOKS. 12mo, 372 pages, with frontispiece. Other stories than the one giving title to the volume are: "The Crazy Professor," "Doña Paula's Treasure," "The Don of Pauper Alley," "The Arrival of the Magpie," and "La Tiburona." These stories are all true to life, and perfectly preserve the atmosphere of the localities in which the scenes are laid. We believe that in interest and literary quality they will not fall below the work done by our most popular writers. Cloth, $1.00; paper, 50 cents.

Tenting on the Plains.—By MRS. ELIZABETH CUSTER, author of "Boots and Saddles." New cheap edition. 12mo, 403 pages, with illustrations. This book was originally published in a very expensive edition and sold only by subscription. Many people who had read and enjoyed "Boots and Saddles" were anxious to read Mrs. Custer's next book, but were deterred by the high price of the book. This new edition is now published to meet this demand. It contains all the illustrations of the more expensive edition, is printed from new plates, and has an attractive new cover. Cloth, $1.00.

AFTERWORD

M. Thomas Inge

When readers picked up Mark Twain's latest novel, *Tom Sawyer Abroad*, in April of 1894, they found themselves in the first few pages in familiar territory. Despite the preeminence given Tom in the title, it is Huckleberry Finn who tells the story once more in his unselfconscious grand style, even though he had declared at the end of his previous tale that "if I'd a knowed what a trouble it was to make a book I wouldn't a tackled it and ain't agoing to no more."[1] No doubt, Twain enthusiasts were happy to to see this promise broken (though they probably never placed any real faith in the fiction of Huck as author anyway) as Huck begins:

> Do you reckon Tom Sawyer was satisfied after all them adventures? I mean the adventures we had down the river the time we set the nigger Jim free and Tom got shot in the leg. No, he wasn't. It only just pisoned him for more. That was all the effects it had. You see, when we three come back up the river in glory, as you may say, from that long travel, and the village received us with a torchlight procession and speeches, and everybody hurrah'd and shouted, and some got drunk, it made us heroes, and that was what Tom Sawyer had always been hankerin' to be.[2]

What Huck makes explicit is that this book is a sequel to *Adventures of Huckleberry Finn*, just as that work made clear in its first paragraph that it was a sequel to an earlier one: "You don't know about me, without you have read a book by the name of 'The Adventures of Tom Sawyer,' but that ain't no matter."[3] It's no matter because all three narratives may be read independently of each other, but we are also compelled to recognize the fact that Twain is developing a series which banks for its appeal on our prior familiarity with Tom, Huck, and Jim.

To put it baldly, Twain is making capital out of his characters and using some of the best-loved figures in American literary history for crass commercial purposes. He didn't want to let some good cash cows go unmilked. This is not the kind of talk and *Tom Sawyer Abroad* is not the kind of book modern critical canonists care to hear about, because it displays a side of Twain's career and intentions of which we have lost sight. After Twain's death in 1910, the critical establishment set about rescuing him for posterity by making out a case for him as more than a "mere" popular humorist and declaring him a writer of high seriousness and aesthetic purpose. Their main exhibit was *Adventures of Huckleberry Finn*, with all its display of stylistic complexity and concern with social and metaphysical themes, such as racism, civil restraint, hypocrisy, freedom, and personal identity. *Huckleberry Finn* demonstrated that serious fiction could be made out of the American experience and couched in the vernacular of the American people.

Formalist critics found in the novel the kind of structure and character development which enabled them to admire it as a well-wrought work, although they were at a loss to explain the seeming lapse, at the end, back into the hypocritical world from which Huck had apparently rescued himself. *Tom Sawyer Abroad* helps explain that lapse. Twain was not about seeking the immortal respect of literary critics, or "crickets," as he called them, but about making a buck with his best available skills and literary capital. If his work turned out to have artistic merit too, so much the better. No wonder most Twain scholars have found *Tom Sawyer Abroad* inferior. Reading it returns us fully into the popular culture of the nineteenth century in which Twain flourished and thrived. While Twain earned and deserves our respect as an author of great range and talent, he was also a writer of and for the people who knew how to strike a chord among his readers. But he did not always succeed.

Twain's commercial intentions are clear not only in his explicit connections between *The Adventures of Tom Sawyer*, *Adventures of Huckleberry Finn*, and *Tom Sawyer Abroad* but also in his vision of this last work as the first of another series which could be continued indefinitely. As he wrote Fred J. Hall, who managed his publishing firm, he planned to send Huck, Tom, and Jim off to other parts of the world "by adding 'Africa,' 'England,' 'Germany,' etc. to the title page of each successive volume of the series."[4] Books in series were all the rage at the time, such as the Peter Parley tales by Samuel G. Goodrich, the Rollo stories by Jacob Abbott, the Elsie Dinsmore books by Martha F. Finley, or the Uncle Remus collections by Joel Chandler Harris. These were primarily books for children, but Twain saw the market for his series as much broader: "I conceive that the right way to write a story for boys is to write so that it will not only interest boys but will strongly interest *any man who has ever been a boy*. That immensely *enlarges the audience*."[5]

That Twain was attuned to the popular literary marketplace is also demonstrated by the sources he looked to for ideas. In addition to *The Arabian Nights*, Sir Walter Scott's *The Talisman*, and the Bible, which appear to have been sources for scenes and incidents, Twain leaned most on Jules Verne. The Frenchman's extremely popular semi-scientific adventure novels were reaching even wider audiences through the English translations of such works as *Twenty Thousand Leagues Under the Sea* (1869–70) and *Around the World in Eighty Days* (1873). But the book to which Twain turned as he wrote *Tom Sawyer Abroad* was Verne's *Five Weeks in a Balloon* (1863). Shortly before the English version appeared in 1869, Twain had started writing a story about the trip "of a man in a balloon from Paris over India, China, Pacific Ocean, the plains to a prairie in Illinois." After a few pages, Twain abruptly stopped and noted, "While this was being written, Jules Verne's 'Five Weeks in a Balloon' came out and consequently this sketch wasn't finished."[6]

The idea persisted. When he returned to it in 1892, he showed no hesitation in borrowing extensively from the book which had stalled him earlier, perhaps because his own ideas became confused with Verne's during the lapse of almost a quarter century. Parallels, in addition to the plot device of a lengthy trip in a balloon, include the use of the word "aeronaut" (in Tom's poor spelling "erronort"), a thirsty trip across the Sahara Desert in search of an oasis, meetings with caravans which bring unwanted attention, an experience with a killing sandstorm, an infant's rescue from bandits and return to its mother in the case of Twain and the rescue of a French missionary in Verne, the observation of a bloody battle from the air, the accidental death of a man who falls overboard, encounters with wild animals on the ground, and other striking incidents. Both novels have three main characters who differ from each other in similar ways in terms of personalities and attributes.[7] Consciously or unconsciously Twain had simply remembered some of the elements that made Jules Verne's book so exciting, and had recycled them for his own purposes. In style and execution, however, *Tom Sawyer Abroad* is entirely Mark Twain's.

Twain began writing *Tom Sawyer Abroad* during a time of great personal and financial distress. His investment in the Paige typesetting machine was proving an enormous drain, to the tune of more than $3,000 a month over a period of several years. His publishing firm, Webster and Company, was absorbing his profits through unsold stock, operating expenses, and production costs for the multivolume *Library of American Literature*, edited by Edmund C. Stedman. His spirits oppressed by the deaths of his and Livy's mothers in 1890, Livy's developing heart trouble, and his own debilitating rheumatism, he closed his Hartford home and moved the family to Europe in hopes of rest cures and lower expenses. After settling in Bad Nauheim in Germany in August of 1892, he began work on the manuscript about the fifth of the month, by the tenth had 12,000 words, and was halfway through two weeks later. Only a month in the making, the book was complete by September 4. Twain ascribed the extraordinary speed to inspiration from which "the humor flows as easily as the adventures and surprises."[8] On the very day that *Tom Sawyer Abroad* was entered for copyright, April 18, 1894, Webster and Company declared bankruptcy. Thus it was the last book issued by that ill-fated firm.

Perhaps because of the collapse of the publisher, no review copies were sent out. That would explain the absolute silence that greeted *Tom Sawyer Abroad* in the American press; at any rate, not a single review has been discovered. However, something happened to the text that suggests this was just as well, a kind of unlucky accident that often bedeviled Twain. The heavy hand of censorship fell upon *Tom Sawyer Abroad* in the person of one of the

spiritual descendants of Thomas Bowdler, popular children's writer Mary
Mapes Dodge.

As the author of *Hans Brinker, or, The Silver Skates* (1865), Mrs. Dodge
had achieved a reputation which also brought her the editorship of the newly
founded *St. Nicholas* magazine for children in 1873. Determined to add to her
distinguished list of contributors, which already included such people as
Rudyard Kipling, Robert Louis Stevenson, and Louisa May Alcott, she
offered Twain $5,000 in the summer of 1892 for first publication rights to a
story appropriate for her young readers at least 50,000 words long. That fall,
in need of all the cash he could raise, he remembered her offer. At first he tried
to negotiate a higher fee, even though *Tom Sawyer Abroad* was only 40,000
words long, and he submitted it to several other children's and general interest magazines as well, but finally he agreed to accept $4,000 from Mrs.
Dodge. The book was serialized in *St. Nicholas* magazine in six consecutive
issues from November 1893 to April 1894.

Having had the original manuscript typed, Twain revised it, sent it to Mrs.
Dodge, and held the carbon for his British publisher, Chatto and Windus.
What Mrs. Dodge set about doing to the text is evident in the very first paragraph. Here is a transcription of the paragraph as found in the manuscript,
with Mrs. Dodge's changes as indicated.

> Do you reckon Tom Sawyer was satisfied after all them adventures? I mean
> the adventures we had down the river [and] the time we set the ~~nigger~~
> [darky] Jim free and Tom got shot in the leg. No, he wasn't. It only just
> ~~pisoned~~ [p'isoned] him for more. That was all the ~~effects~~ [effect] it had.
> You see, when we three ~~come~~ [came] back up the river in glory, as you may
> say, from that long travel, and the village received us with a torchlight pro-
> cession and speeches, and everybody hurrah'd and shouted, ~~and some got~~
> ~~drunk~~, it made us heroes, and that was what Tom Sawyer had always been
> ~~sweating~~ [hankering] to be.[9]

Just six editorial changes and deletions, really, but a few of them speak loudly
for Mrs. Dodge's attitudes about what was appropriate for children to read.

Already attuned to the most controversial word in the entire Twain canon, she removed "nigger" here and everywhere else in the manuscript, except for an occasion when Jim refers to himself that way, and replaced it with "darky." The idea of a crowd of drunks greeting the adventurers offended her, as did Tom's sweat. There would be no drinking or sweating in the polite pages of *St. Nicholas* magazine. Huck's dialect was acceptable, although she had to touch up the usage just a bit. These changes were emblematic of the others that followed as the installments appeared: the language corrected and slightly elevated, drinking and vulgar actions banished, sweating and bodily functions eliminated, and no racial epithets allowed. Criticisms of specific religious groups were banned, from Roman Catholicism to Presbyterianism, including Bible and Sunday school lessons. Because the narrative deals so frequently with death, and often in very vivid terms, she was unable to remove all the references, but she valiantly deleted as many as she could without losing sense. Even a bird sitting on a "dead limb" had to go.[10]

In his introduction to the Mark Twain Project edition of *Tom Sawyer Abroad*, John C. Gerber notes that what Twain had to say "about the mayhem Mrs. Dodge committed on his narrative is not recorded."[11] The comments of Twain's illustrator, Daniel Carter Beard, however, are. As Beard tells it in his autobiography,

When Mark Twain sent the manuscript in, there were some parts of it or a part of it which Mary Mapes Dodge thought that she could improve, and the wording was changed. Mark Twain was a kindly soul, a gentle soul, but if Roosevelt stood for civic righteousness, Mark Twain stood for literary righteousness, and the unalienable rights of the author. When he read the proof with the changed wording in it, he was wroth, and, entering the sanctum sanctorium [*sic*], the holy of holies, the editorial department of "St. Nicholas," he shocked the gentle creatures and terrified the associate editors by exclaiming, "Any editor to whom I submit my manuscripts has an undisputed right to delete anything to which he objects, but!" and his brows knit as he said it, "God Almighty himself can't put words in my mouth that I did not use!"

After smelling-salts were administered to the whole editorial corps, and Mary Mapes Dodge was resuscitated by Mr. Clark, the mistake was remedied, the error was rectified, and things went smoothly. I was not present, but some of the editorial staff themselves told me of the incident as a profound secret, which I have not divulged until this present moment.[12]

The above quotation comes not from Beard's published autobiography, *Hardly a Man Is Now Alive*, but from the fuller unedited version in his manuscripts at the Library of Congress. The editors removed Mrs. Dodge's name from the published book and thus, ironically, exercised on Beard a degree of the expurgation practiced on Twain. Also omitted were three subsequent paragraphs detailing other examples of Mrs. Dodge's expurgations; for instance, she had the udders removed from Beard's drawing of a cow because "they were very vulgar," with the result that "there was no way of telling whether it was a steer, a cow, or a bull."

There may be a degree of exaggeration in this secondhand report, since Beard was prone to exaggeration when he wrote about his friend Mark Twain, and it was not simply one mistake but the editing of the entire manuscript that would have upset the author. But there must be some truth in the story since Beard knew the staff at *St. Nicholas* and had a personal stake in this very project which would cause him to experience Mrs. Dodge's purifying judgment as well. Beard had been the illustrator of *A Connecticut Yankee in King Arthur's Court* in 1889, and Twain had praised him lavishly as "the only man who can correctly illustrate my writings, for he not only illustrates the text but he illustrates my thoughts."[13] Twain must have been pleased, then, to find Beard in charge of the drawings for the serialization. In his account of Twain's angry visit to the offices of *St. Nicholas*, Beard continued:

What prompted them [the editorial staff] to give [me] this confidential information was that my illustrations of Huck Finn, Tom Sawyer and Nigger Jim had been returned to me because Mary Mapes Dodge had ruled that it was vulgar to depict them with *bare feet!* and I was asked to put shoes on them. Of course, I was working for "St. Nicholas," and it was only right that I should conform to St. Nicholas's idea of propriety, so I pinched the toes of those poor vagabonds with shoes, mentally asking forgiveness as I did so.[14]

In the first drawing Beard did for the serialization (19), the artist took his revenge for having to put shoes on Huck by leaving the shoelaces untied.

Beard did complete satisfactorily and with shoes twenty-eight illustrations for the magazine, with twenty-six being carried over to the published book and two new drawings as chapter ending devices. In general, the illustrations nowhere near match those for *A Connecticut Yankee* in style, detail, or dramatic action; they settle for reflecting the text rather than interpreting it. One of them, however, has a special interest. The last chapter of the book includes a "Map of the Trip made by Tom Sawyer, Erronort, 1850," which traces the travels of the balloon from the United States to and across Africa (215). Beard drew it in the style of Tom Sawyer but based it on a version drawn by Mark Twain. The author roughed out the map on tracing paper for Beard to follow, and the original is preserved among Beard's papers at the Library of Congress, with his signed notation, "This is the map drawn by Mark Twain."[15] Thus we have one more example of Twain's fairly undistinguished attempts at drawing.

What happened next in the publishing history of *Tom Sawyer Abroad* remains unclear. Twain's intention to use the unexpurgated text in the American edition is explicit in a letter to Fred J. Hall: "Use the original — not the *St. Nicholas* version of '*TOM SAWYER ABROAD.*'"[16] Despite this instruction, somehow the typesetter used the *St. Nicholas* text for the first two-thirds of the American edition but then switched to the original typescript for the last third, chapters 10 through 13. There was some confusion in the offices of Chatto and Windus too. They wrote to Hall on January 16, 1894, that they had in hand the first seven chapters of the book as published in *St. Nicholas* and awaited the remainder to begin setting type.[17] Apparently the carbon of Twain's typescript reached them in good time, since that was the copy text for the British edition. Thus, while Americans read mainly the Mary Mapes

Dodge sanitized and starched *Tom Sawyer Abroad*, British readers got direct, unadulterated, hundred-proof Twain. The author's opinion of this state of affairs was presumably lost in the rumble of a collapsing publishing firm.

Had there been any American reviews, they might not have been much different from the British, except for one consideration. Still smarting from the treatment of British culture and attitudes in *A Connecticut Yankee in King Arthur's Court* five years earlier, British reviewers were not entirely hospitable to new books by Twain. The reviewer for the *Academy*, the Shakespearean R. K. Chambers, was relieved that Twain had directed his satiric glance elsewhere: "It is more decent to parody Jules Verne than Sir Thomas Malory, and Mark Twain may therefore be deemed to have returned in his latest flight of humour to the limits of legitimate burlesque." But in this case the humor was flat: "The chief fault of the book is that it does not strike one as particularly funny, which is perhaps a considerable defect in what is professedly a work of humour."[18]

Likewise, the *Athenaeum* noted that the well-loved Huck and Tom had in this book "lost nearly all their fun," and that "Mark Twain has often proved that he has the gift of being amusing; it is a pity that he should squander himself on such a book as this."[19] The *Bookman* believed that the various adventures, with their "incongruity of American new humour meeting African barbarism and strangeness, hardly do more than provoke a wearied smile."[20] The *Spectator* simply noted that the new book was no match for the earlier adventures of Tom Sawyer.[21] Perhaps the London *Saturday Review* most wittily summed up the British response in the first paragraph of its notice:

If the image be not too domestic a one, we would say that in *Tom Sawyer Abroad* the tea is of the best Mark Twain brand, but that the teapot has been watered. The humour is genuine and characteristic, but it is thin. Not here are to be tasted the first sprightly runnings of *The Innocents Abroad*, nor, on the other hand, that distasteful blend displayed in *A Yankee at the Court of King Arthur* [the British title]. We are amused and gratified, but not to a sufficient extent. As Raleigh said of the sack they gave him on the way to the scaffold, "It is good drink, if a man might stay by it." *Tom Sawyer*

Abroad is good fun, but we are afraid that we shall not stay by it; we have an impression that a year hence we shall be as if we had not read it.

But by the end of the lengthy review, the critic admitted that many of "the incidents are mildly but distinctly amusing, and there are delicious passages of Twainian philosophy."[22]

A few months after this initial reaction, a more carefully considered review appeared in the *Pall Mall Magazine*, by one I. Zangwill, who took note of "not a few memorable passages," as well as a frequent "delicious stroke of humour" and "a flash of the old genius." Zangwill paid one high compliment in remarking that Twain "is quite as much set upon scarifying the superstitions of his day as Rabelais, with the versatility of whose life, by the way, his own has had a curious affinity."[23]

The estimates of Twain scholars over the years have also been mixed. John C. Gerber, who has written more extensively about *Tom Sawyer Abroad* than any other, has found it "witty but elementary" and "arbitrarily contrived," but not to "be casually dismissed as second rate."[24] Biographer Everett Emerson called the story "flawed" and "a disappointment, despite some amusing touches," but finally found a place for it on his list of Twain's "neglected works that deserve a reading."[25] William Gibson placed it among Twain's "undistinguished" books, yet he also praised it as "the brightest, most continually entertaining of the fictions" about Tom, Huck, and Jim.[26] The book's most ardent defender was Bernard DeVoto, who thought it a brilliant exploration of "ignorant thought" and "the backwoods mind," and "an elaborate exposition of St. Petersburg trying to grapple with an enlargement of its thinking." "There can be no doubt," he concluded, "that Mark Twain's deliberate effort was to explore the mentality of the common man."[27]

DeVoto thus touched on one of the strengths of the book, that is, the numerous and detailed conversations that take place among the three comrades during the course of the balloon journey. Listening (and one does indeed "hear" them) to Huck Finn's untutored common sense and Jim's naive but sound logic come up against the rational but romatic arguments of Tom Sawyer is one of the delights of the book. While the plot follows its inevitable course according to the dictates of wind and geography, the conversation ranges over a multiplicity of topics, including the Crusades, the nature of genius, physical geography, the limitations of maps, time zones, realism in painting, metaphorical language, the art of cursing, the origin of deserts, racial discrimination, religious toleration, and the relationship of speed, strength, and physical size in nature. When Tom loses his patience and shouts, "Oh, shut your head! you make me tired. I don't want to argue no more with people like you," Huck calmly and reasonably comments:

> Now that's just where Tom Sawyer warn't fair. Jim didn't mean no harm, and I didn't mean no harm. We knowed well enough that he was right and we was wrong, and all that we was after was to get at the how of it, that's all; and the only reason he couldn't explain it so we could understand it was because we was ignorant — yes, and pretty dull, too, I ain't denying that; but land! that ain't no crime, I should think.[28]

Such fair-minded humility brings us over to Huck's side in these arguments as we perceive that his heart is in the right place, however benighted his head may be. We've seen that before.

Huck also holds forth once again on his problems with civilization and the constraints it places on his behavior. In one passage he takes a page out of Henry David Thoreau's *Walden* (the chapter "Where I Lived, and What I Lived for") to castigate the advances in modern communication.

> Now, one of the worst things about civilization is, that anybody that gets a letter with trouble in it comes and tells you all about it and makes you feel bad, and the newspapers fetches you the troubles of everybody all over the world, and keeps you down-hearted and dismal most all the time, and its such a heavy load for a person. I hate them newspapers; and I hate letters; and if I had my way I wouldn't allow nobody to load his troubles onto other folks he ain't acquainted with, on t'other side of the world, that way.[29]

But those readers expecting a fully enlightened Huck, regenerated in the power of his grace and humanity through his willingness to sacrifice his soul for Jim, will be disappointed. As in the last chapters of his own book, Huck slips back into his mindless and slavish worship of Tom's conscienceless imagination.

Twain's comic talent shines forth on many of the pages of *Tom Sawyer Abroad*. For example, the story told by Nat Parsons about his trip to Washington in the first chapter is frontier humor at its best, hilarious and outrageous, and one of hundreds of such stories about the country bumpkin come to town.[30] Many of Twain's familiar comic sayings are found here: "the person that had took a bull by the tail once had learned sixty or seventy times as much as a person that hadn't; and . . . a person that started in to carry a cat home by the tail was gitting knowledge that was always going to be useful to him, and wasn't ever going to grow dim or doubtful";[31] or "for all the brag you hear about knowledge being such a wonderful thing, instink is worth forty of it for real unerringness."[32] This is prime Twain, although he is equally capable of descending to the lowest kind of pun to get a cheap laugh, as in "Mary had a little lamb, its fleas was white as snow."[33]

If, as I have suggested, Twain's interests were primarily commercial in writing *Tom Sawyer Abroad*, he was to a certain extent successful even though the planned series remained unwritten. It was fifth among all his books in total sales before 1930, went through seven American editions by 1970, and appeared in another nineteen editions along with *Tom Sawyer, Detective* and other stories. Two separate and eight combined editions appeared in England, and it has proven popular in several foreign language translations, including German, French, and Spanish.[34] What the critics have largely disdained, then, has been embraced by the public for whom Twain wrote. But anyone is likely to find more than a few laughs between the covers of *Tom Sawyer Abroad*.

NOTES

1. Mark Twain, *Adventures of Huckleberry Finn*, ed. Walter Blair and Victor Fischer (Berkeley: University of California Press, 1985), p. 362.

2. Mark Twain, *The Adventures of Tom Sawyer, Tom Sawyer Abroad, Tom Sawyer, Detec-*

tive, ed. John C. Gerber, Paul Baender, and Terry Firkins (Berkeley: University of California Press, 1980), p. 255; cited hereafter as *Tom Sawyer Abroad*.

3. *Adventures of Huckleberry Finn*, p. 1.

4. Cited in John C. Gerber, introduction to *Tom Sawyer Abroad*, pp. 245–46.

5. Gerber, p. 246.

6. Cited in D. M. McKeithan, "Mark Twain's *Tom Sawyer Abroad* and Jules Verne's *Five Weeks in a Balloon*," *Texas Studies in English*, 28 (1949), 257.

7. These parallels are outlined fully in McKeithan, pp. 257–70.

8. Gerber, p. 246.

9. The manuscript version is cited from O M Brack, Jr., "Mark Twain in Knee Pants: The Expurgation of *Tom Sawyer Abroad*," *Proof*, 2 (1972), 147–48.

10. Mrs. Dodge's changes are fully and carefully documented in Brack, pp. 145–51.

11. Gerber, p. 248.

12. Undated typescript in the Daniel Carter Beard Collection, Manuscripts Division, Library of Congress, Box 241. Cf. Dan Beard, *Hardly a Man Is Now Alive* (New York: Doubleday, Doran, 1939), p. 344.

13. See M. Thomas Inge, "Mark Twain and Dan Beard's Collaborative *Connecticut Yankee*," in *Author-ity and Textuality: Current Views of Collaborative Writing*, ed. James S. Leonard, Christine E. Wharton, Robert Murray Davis, and Jeanette Harris (West Cornwall, Conn.: Locust Hill Press, 1994), pp. 169–227.

14. Undated typescript, Beard Collection, Library of Congress. Cf. Beard, pp. 344–45.

15. Unpublished drawing in the Daniel Carter Beard Collection, Manuscripts Division, Library of Congress, Box 35.

16. Gerber, p. 624.

17. Cited in Sidney Berger, "New Mark Twain Items," *Papers of the Bibliographical Society of America*, 68 (1974), 331–35.

18. R. K. Chambers, *Academy* no. 1158 (July 14, 1894), 27.

19. *Athenaeum* no. 3474 (May 26, 1894), 676.

20. *Bookman*, 6 (June 1894), 89–90.

21. *Spectator*, 72 (June 2, 1894), 764.

22. *Saturday Review*, 77 (May 19, 1894), 535–36.

23. I. Zangwill, *Pall Mall Magazine*, 4 (November 1894), 524–25.

24. Gerber, p. 242, and "*Tom Sawyer Abroad*," in *The Mark Twain Encyclopedia*, ed. J. R. LeMaster and James D. Wilson (New York: Garland, 1993), pp. 739–40.

25. Everett Emerson, *The Authentic Mark Twain* (Philadelphia: University of Pennsylvania Press, 1984), pp. 203, 180, and 277.

26. William M. Gibson, *The Art of Mark Twain* (New York: Oxford University Press, 1976), pp. 98 and 158.

27. Bernard DeVoto, *Mark Twain's America* (Boston: Little, Brown, 1932), p. 302.

28. *Tom Sawyer Abroad*, pp. 261–62.

29. *Tom Sawyer Abroad*, p. 294.

30. Parsons' story was first thought to have been borrowed from an episode in *Roughing It* (1872), but Earl F. Briden in "The Sources of Nat Parsons's Tale in *Tom Sawyer Abroad*," *ANQ*, 6 (January 1993), 18–20, has located its source in two anecdotes, one recorded in Twain's notebooks and the other in *Life on the Mississippi* (1883).

31. *Tom Sawyer Abroad*, p. 316.

32. *Tom Sawyer Abroad*, p. 337.

33. *Tom Sawyer Abroad*, p. 286.

34. Gerber, p. 250.

FOR FURTHER READING

M. Thomas Inge

Useful information on the background, composition, and reception of *Tom Sawyer Abroad* can be found in the introductions and editorial apparatus by John C. Gerber, Paul Baender, and Terry Firkins for *The Adventures of Tom Sawyer, Tom Sawyer Abroad, Tom Sawyer, Detective* (Berkeley: University of California Press, 1980); Everett Emerson's *The Authentic Mark Twain* (Philadelphia: University of Pennsylvania Press, 1984); William M. Gibson's *The Art of Mark Twain* (New York: Oxford University Press, 1976); Louis J. Budd's *Mark Twain: Social Philosopher* (Bloomington: Indiana University Press, 1962); and *The Mark Twain Encyclopedia*, edited by J. R. LeMaster and James D. Wilson (New York: Garland, 1993).

The textual history of the novel and its expurgation are thoroughly analyzed by O M Brack, Jr., in "Mark Twain in Knee Pants: The Expurgation of *Tom Sawyer Abroad*," *Proof* 2 (1972), 145–51. Source studies include Earl F. Briden, "The Sources of Nat Parsons's Tale in *Tom Sawyer Abroad*," *ANQ*, 6 (January 1993), 18–20; Carl Isler, "Mark Twain's Style," *Mark Twain Journal*, 18 (Summer 1976), 18–19; D. M. McKeithan, "Mark Twain's *Tom Sawyer Abroad* and Jules Verne's *Five Weeks in a Balloon*," *Texas Studies in English*, 28 (1949), 257–70; and Chadwick Hansen, "There Weren't No Home Like a Raft Floating Down the Mississippi, or Like a Raft Floating Down the Neckar, or Like a Balloon Across the Sahara: Mark Twain as Improviser," in *Directions in Literary Criticism*, ed. Stanley Weintraub and Philip Young (University Park: Penn State University Press, 1973), 160–67.

Twain's friendship with the illustrator is recounted in Dan Beard's *Hardly a Man Is Now Alive* (New York: Doubleday, Doran, 1939), and M. Thomas Inge, "Mark Twain and Dan Beard's Collaborative *Connecticut Yankee*," in *Author-ity and Textuality: Current Views of Collaborative Writing*, ed. James S. Leonard and others (West Cornwall, Conn: Locust Hill Press, 1994), 169–227.

Tom Sawyer Abroad was partially adapted in Will Vinton's claymation animated feature film *The Adventures of Mark Twain by Huck Finn* (Clubhouse Pictures and Paramount Home Video, VHS #2376, 1986).

ILLUSTRATORS AND ILLUSTRATIONS
IN MARK TWAIN'S FIRST AMERICAN EDITIONS

Beverly R. David & Ray Sapirstein

From the "gorgeous gold frog" stamped into the cover of *The Celebrated Jumping Frog of Calaveras County* in 1867 to the comet-riding captain on the frontispiece of *Extract from Captain Stormfield's Visit to Heaven* in 1909, illustrators and illustrations were an integral part of Mark Twain's first editions.

Twain marketed most of his major works by subscription, and illustration functioned as an important sales tool. Subscription books were packed with pictures of every type and size and were bound in brassy gold-stamped covers. The books were sold by agents who flipped through a prospectus filled with lively illustrations, selected text, and binding samples. Illustrations quickly conveyed a sense of the story, condensing the proverbial "thousand words" and outlining the scope and tone of the work, making an impression on the potential purchaser even before the full text had been printed. Book canvassers were rewarded with up to 50 percent of the selling price, which started at $3.50 and ranged as high as $7.00 for more ornate bindings. The books themselves were seldom produced until a substantial number of customers had placed orders. To justify the relatively high price and to reassure buyers that they were getting their money's worth, books published by subscription had to offer sensational volume and apparent substance. As Frank Bliss of the American Publishing Company observed, these consumers "would not pay for blank paper and wide margins. They wanted everything filled up with type or pictures." While authors of trade books generally tolerated lighter sales, gratified by attracting a "better class of readers," as Hamlin Hill put it, authors of subscription books sacrificed literary respectability for popular appeal and considerable profit.[1]

The humorist George Ade remembered Twain's books vividly, offering us a child's-eye view of the nineteenth-century subscription book market.

Just when front-room literature seemed at its lowest ebb, so far as the American boy was concerned, along came Mark Twain. His books looked at a distance, just like the other distended, diluted, and altogether tasteless volumes that had been used for several decades to balance the ends of the center table . . . so thick and heavy and emblazoned with gold that [they] could keep company with the bulky and high-priced Bible. . . . The publisher knew his public, so he gave a pound of book for every fifty cents, and crowded in plenty of wood-cuts and stamped the outside with golden bouquets and put in a steel engraving of the author, with a tissue paper veil over it, and "sicked" his multitude of broken-down clergymen, maiden ladies, grass widows, and college students on the great American public.

Can you see the boy, Sunday morning prisoner, approach the book with a dull sense of foreboding, expecting a dose of Tupper's *Proverbial Philosophy*? Can you see him a few minutes later when he finds himself linked arm-in-arm with Mulberry Sellers or Buck Fanshaw or the convulsing idiot who wanted to know if Christopher Columbus was sure-enough dead? No wonder he curled up on the hair-cloth sofa and hugged the thing to his bosom and lost all interest in Sunday school. *Innocents Abroad* was the most enthralling book ever printed until *Roughing It* appeared. Then along came *The Gilded Age*, *Life on the Mississippi*, and *Tom Sawyer*. . . . While waiting for a new one we read the old ones all over again.[2]

Publishers, editors, and Twain himself spent a good deal of time on design — choosing the most talented artists, directing their interpretations of text, selecting from the final prints, and at times removing material they deemed unfit for illustration.[3]

With the exception of *Following the Equator* (1897), books released in the twilight of Twain's career were not sold by subscription. Twain's later books, published for the trade market by Harper and Brothers, seldom contained more than a frontispiece and a dozen or so tasteful illustrations, rather than the hundreds of illustrations per volume that subscription publishing demanded. Illustration, however, remained a major component of Twain's later work in two important cases: *Extracts from Adam's Diary*, illustrated by Fred

Strothmann in 1904, and *Eve's Diary*, illustrated by Lester Ralph in 1906.

The stories behind the illustrators and illustrations of Mark Twain's first editions abound in back-room intrigue. The besotted or negligent lapses of some of the artists and the procrastinations of the engravers are legendary. The consequent production delays, mistimed releases, and copyright infringements all implied a lack of competent supervision that frequently infuriated Twain and ultimately encouraged him to launch his own publishing company.

In many cases, Twain took illustrations into account as he wrote and edited his text, using them as counterpoint and accompaniment to his words, often allowing them to inform his general narrative strategy and to influence the amount of detail he felt necessary to include in his written descriptions. In the most artful and carefully considered illustrated works, an analysis of the relationships between author and illustrator and between text and pictures illuminates key dimensions of Twain's writings and the responses they have elicited from readers. Examinations of even the most straightforward examples of decorative imagery yield insights into the publishing history of Twain's books and his attitudes toward the production process.

The original illustrations in Twain's works have often been replaced in the twentieth century by subsequent visual interpretations. But while Norman Rockwell's well-known nostalgic renderings of *Tom Sawyer* and *Huckleberry Finn* may tell us much about 1930s sensibilities, we would do well to reacquaint ourselves with the first American editions and the artwork they contained if we want to understand the books Twain wrote and the world they affected.

Illustrated books, like the illustrated weekly magazines that first appeared in the 1860s, were a significant source of visual images entering nineteenth-century homes. Because of their widespread popularity and the relative paucity of other sources of visual information, Twain's books helped to define America's perceptions of remote people, exotic scenes, and historic events. In addition to being an essential element of Mark Twain's body of work, illustrations are a documentary source in their own right, a window into Twain's world and our own.

NOTES

1. For background on subscription book publishing, see Hamlin Hill, *Mark Twain and Elisha Bliss* (Columbia: University of Missouri Press, 1964), chapter 1. See also R. Kent Rasmussen, "Subscription-book publishing" entry, *Mark Twain A to Z: The Essential Reference to His Life and Writings* (New York: Facts on File, 1995), p. 448.

2. George Ade, "Mark Twain and the Old-Time Subscription Book," *Review of Reviews* 61 (June 10, 1910): 703–4; reprinted in Frederick Anderson, ed., *Mark Twain: The Critical Heritage* (London: Routledge and Kegan Paul, 1971), pp. 337–39.

3. Beverly R. David, *Mark Twain and His Illustrators, Volume 1 (1869–1875)* (Troy, N.Y.: Whitston Publishing Company, 1986), discusses in detail Twain's involvement in the production of his early books.

READING THE ILLUSTRATIONS IN *TOM SAWYER ABROAD*

Beverly R. David & Ray Sapirstein

When Mary Mapes Dodge, editor in chief of the children's magazine *St. Nicholas*, expressed interest in acquiring serial rights to publish *Tom Sawyer Abroad* in installments, Mark Twain attempted to cleanse his manuscript of anything that might excite subscribers' protective concern for the welfare of young morals. He wrote Fred Hall, his manager and partner in the publishing firm Charles L. Webster and Company, that he had "tried to leave the improprieties all out; if I didn't, Mrs. Dodge can scissor them out."[1] Despite Twain's careful grooming of the manuscript, Dodge excised over two thousand words, deleting references to profanity, death, religion, and perspiration.[2]

Twain was surely pleased to learn that Dodge had selected Dan Beard to illustrate the series. Beard (1850–1941) had worked for Twain before, most notably on *A Connecticut Yankee in King Arthur's Court*. There Twain had enthusiastically allowed the artist free rein to construct a kindred yet independent complement to the book's narrative, and had expressed his admiration for and trust in Beard as a conscientious and creative collaborator. An uninhibited and energetic humorist himself, Beard too ran afoul of *St. Nicholas*'s editorial sensitivities. He later wrote that his illustrations of Huck, Tom, and Jim for *Tom Sawyer Abroad* were

> returned to me, the editor ruling that it was excessively coarse and vulgar to depict them with *bare feet*! I was asked to cover their nakedness with shoes . . . so I pinched the toes of those poor vagabonds with shoes they never wore in life, mentally asking their forgiveness as I did so.[3]

Beard found it necessary to depart from the text in another area. Dissatisfied with Twain's mating of a dirigible with a flying machine, he decided to fashion his own airship in the illustrations, reasoning that "Mark Twain hadn't made an exhaustive study of aviation, bless his soul."[4] Twain's stubbornly evasive description of the ship's design and propulsion demanded a convincing rendering by the illustrator. However, despite Beard's "research" in aviation, his quaintly nautical, batwinged, Leonardo-like flying machine hardly seems airworthy to today's eyes.

In 1894, Twain's publishing house released *Tom Sawyer Abroad* as a book, illustrated with twenty-seven drawings Beard had completed for *St. Nicholas*. The cover reproduced the line drawing "Run! Run Fo' Yo' Life" (69) in color, stamped in black and dull orange on tan cloth, featuring Tom and Huck dashing toward the reader from one of Twain's ridiculously savage lions. Although Twain's descriptions of animal behavior may have been more fantastic than factual, Beard evidently studied the variety of creatures he depicted, and drew them with careful anatomical realism. The male lions snapping at Huck as he hangs from the ship's ladder (77) resemble a group of motion studies, though Beard invested their facial expressions with humor. His series of giant fleas (99, 107, 111), including the satirical and precisely rendered potbellied presidential flea, probably reflected hours of copying from scientific books, or even firsthand microscopic observation. While the images Beard found challenging — images of exotic animals and peoples — are successful, the main characters often appear uncharacteristically primitive, perhaps an indication of his frustration with editorial meddling and interminable revision. His folksy drawing of the three heroes, elegantly dressed in the professor's "starchiest duds" and dancing on the deck of the ship (175), displays awkwardly proportioned figures and angular postures, although its boyish scribble exudes humor and easy triumph. The three reach their pinnacle of smug gaudiness in "Rescue of Jim" (199), clad like children playing dress-up in an attic adventure. Overall, Beard's images are uneven, alternating between detailed pen-and-ink drawings and washy halftones, but lending the book a spontaneous and whimsical air that befits Huck's narrative voice.

Twain himself contributed to one of the illustrations in the book. As was his custom by this time in his career, he provided a hand-drawn map of the journey when he submitted the manuscript to Webster and Company. Beard saved the drawing and used it for reference to produce the map that appears on page 215. He followed Twain's original closely, adding tiny scenic details and characters.

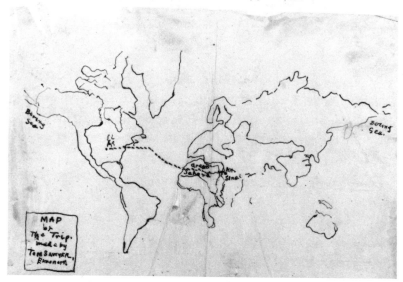

Twain's hand-drawn map of the journey made by Tom Sawyer. (Daniel Carter Beard Papers, container 35. Reproduced from the collections of the Library of Congress.)

Although Twain was upset by the alteration of his text as it appeared in *St. Nicholas*, he thought highly of Beard's illustrations. After reviewing the first installment of the series, he wrote his daughter Clara, "I think Dan Beard's pictures in 'Tom Sawyer Abroad,' in St. Nicholas, are mighty good."[5]

NOTES

1. SLC to Fred J. Hall, October 31, 1892, in *Mark Twain's Letters to His Publishers, 1867–1894*, Hamlin Hill, ed. (Berkeley: University of California Press, 1967), p. 324.

2. Note on the Texts, *The Adventures of Tom Sawyer; Tom Sawyer Abroad; Tom Sawyer, Detective*, ed. John C. Gerber, The Works of Mark Twain (Berkeley: University of California Press, 1982), p. 190.

3. *Hardly a Man Is Now Alive: The Autobiography of Dan Beard* (New York: Doubleday, Doran, and Company, 1939), pp. 344–45.

4. Quoted in Cyril Clemens, "Dan Beard and *A Connecticut Yankee*," *Hobbies* 79 (October 1974): 136.

5. SLC to Clara Clemens, October 16, 1893, cited in Note on the Texts, p. 190.

A NOTE ON THE TEXT

Robert H. Hirst

This text of *Tom Sawyer Abroad by Huck Finn* is a photographic facsimile of a copy of the first American edition dated 1894 on the title page. According to Mark Twain's own statement, the first edition was published in the United States on April 16, 1894. Two copies were deposited with the Copyright Office on April 18, the same day on which the publisher, Charles L. Webster and Company, declared bankruptcy. All known copies are dated 1894 on the title page, at least in part because the plates were assets in the bankruptcy. The copy reproduced here, which was inscribed on May 19, is an example of Jacob Blanck's binding state B. Blanck noted, however, that the two states are of "unknown sequence" (*BAL* 3440). No textual variation was found among the several copies of this edition compared for the Iowa-California critical edition (*The Adventures of Tom Sawyer; Tom Sawyer Abroad; Tom Sawyer, Detective,* ed. John Gerber, Paul Baender, and Terry Firkins, The Works of Mark Twain, University of California Press, 1980, pp. 639–44). The original volume is in the collection of the Mark Twain House in Hartford, Connecticut (810/C625tos/1894/c. 1).

THE MARK TWAIN HOUSE

The Mark Twain House is a museum and research center dedicated to the study of Mark Twain, his works, and his times. The museum is located in the nineteen-room mansion in Hartford, Connecticut, built for and lived in by Samuel L. Clemens, his wife, and their three children, from 1874 to 1891. The Picturesque Gothic-style residence, with interior design by the firm of Louis Comfort Tiffany and Associated Artists, is one of the premier examples of domestic Victorian architecture in America. Clemens wrote *Adventures of Huckleberry Finn*, *The Adventures of Tom Sawyer*, *A Connecticut Yankee in King Arthur's Court*, *The Prince and the Pauper*, and *Life on the Mississippi* while living in Hartford.

The Mark Twain House is open year-round. In addition to tours of the house, the educational programs of the Mark Twain House include symposia, lectures, and teacher training seminars that focus on the contemporary relevance of Twain's legacy. Past programs have featured discussions of literary censorship with playwright Arthur Miller and writer William Styron; of the power of language with journalist Clarence Page, comedian Dick Gregory, and writer Gloria Naylor; and of the challenges of teaching *Adventures of Huckleberry Finn* amidst charges of racism.

CONTRIBUTORS

Beverly R. David is professor emerita of humanities and theater at Western Michigan University in Kalamazoo. She is currently working on volume 2 of *Mark Twain and His Illustrators*, and on a Mark Twain mystery entitled *Murder at the Matterhorn*. She has written a number of sections on illustration for the *Mark Twain Encyclopedia* and her *Mark Twain and His Illustrators, Volume 1 (1869–1875)* was published in 1989. Dr. David resides in Allegan, Michigan, in the summer and Green Valley, Arizona, in the winter.

Shelley Fisher Fishkin, professor of American Studies and English at the University of Texas at Austin, is the author of the award-winning books *Was Huck Black? Mark Twain and African-American Voices* (1993) and *From Fact to Fiction: Journalism and Imaginative Writing in America* (1985). Her most recent book is *Lighting Out for the Territory: Reflections on Mark Twain and American Culture* (1996). She holds a Ph.D. in American Studies from Yale University, has lectured on Mark Twain in Belgium, England, France, Israel, Italy, Mexico, the Netherlands, and Turkey, as well as throughout the United States, and is president-elect of the Mark Twain Circle of America.

Nat Hentoff is a columnist for the *Washington Post* and the *Village Voice*. He holds a B.A. from Northeastern University, attended Harvard University, and studied at the Sorbonne in Paris as a Fulbright fellow. His books include *The Jazz Life* (1961), *Our Children Are Dying* (1966), *Journey into Jazz* (1968), *A Political Life: The Education of John V. Lindsay* (1969), *The First Freedom : The Tumultuous History of Free Speech in America* (1980), *Blues for Charlie Darwin* (1982), *The Day They Came to Arrest the Book* (1982), *Boston Boy: A Memoir* (1986), *Free Speech for Me—But Not for Thee* (1992), and *Listen to the Stories: Nat Hentoff on Jazz and Country Music* (1995). He lectures widely, and lives in New York City.

Robert H. Hirst is the General Editor of the Mark Twain Project at The Bancroft Library, University of California in Berkeley. Apart from that, he has no other known eccentricities.

M. Thomas Inge is Robert Emory Blackwell Professor of Humanities at Randolph-Macon College in Ashland, Virginia. He holds a B.A. in English and Spanish from Randolph-Macon and M.A. and Ph.D. degrees in English and American literature from Vanderbilt University. As a senior Fulbright lecturer, he has taught in Salamanca, Buenos Aires, Moscow, and Prague. He is the editor of *Huck Finn Among the Critics* (1985) and the author of *Comics as Culture* (1990), *Faulkner, Sut, and Other Southerners* (1992), *Perspectives on American Culture* (1994), and *Anything Can Happen in a Comic Strip* (1995), among other books.

Ray Sapirstein is a doctoral student in the American Civilization Program at the University of Texas at Austin. He curated the 1993 exhibition *Another Side of Huckleberry Finn: Mark Twain and Images of African Americans* at the Harry Ransom Humanities Research Center at the University of Texas at Austin. He is currently completing a dissertation on the photographic illustrations in several volumes of Paul Laurence Dunbar's poetry.

ACKNOWLEDGMENTS

There are a number of people without whom The Oxford Mark Twain would not have happened. I am indebted to Laura Brown, senior vice president and trade publisher, Oxford University Press, for suggesting that I edit an "Oxford Mark Twain," and for being so enthusiastic when I proposed that it take the present form. Her guidance and vision have informed the entire undertaking.

Crucial as well, from the earliest to the final stages, was the help of John Boyer, executive director of the Mark Twain House, who recognized the importance of the project and gave it his wholehearted support.

My father, Milton Fisher, believed in this project from the start and helped nurture it every step of the way, as did my stepmother, Carol Plaine Fisher. Their encouragement and support made it all possible. The memory of my mother, Renée B. Fisher, sustained me throughout.

I am enormously grateful to all the contributors to The Oxford Mark Twain for the effort they put into their essays, and for having been such fine, collegial collaborators. Each came through, just as I'd hoped, with fresh insights and lively prose. It was a privilege and a pleasure to work with them, and I value the friendships that we forged in the process.

In addition to writing his fine afterword, Louis J. Budd provided invaluable advice and support, even going so far as to read each of the essays for accuracy. All of us involved in this project are greatly in his debt. Both his knowledge of Mark Twain's work and his generosity as a colleague are legendary and unsurpassed.

Elizabeth Maguire's commitment to The Oxford Mark Twain during her time as senior editor at Oxford was exemplary. When the project proved to be more ambitious and complicated than any of us had expected, Liz helped make it not only manageable, but fun. Assistant editor Elda Rotor's wonderful help in coordinating all aspects of The Oxford Mark Twain, along with literature editor T. Susan Chang's enthusiastic involvement with the project in its final stages, helped bring it all to fruition.

I am extremely grateful to Joy Johannessen for her astute and sensitive copyediting, and for having been such a pleasure to work with. And I appreciate the conscientiousness and good humor with which Kathy Kuhtz Campbell heroically supervised all aspects of the set's production. Oxford president Edward Barry, vice president and editorial director Helen McInnis, marketing director Amy Roberts, publicity director Susan Rotermund, art director David Tran, trade editorial, design and production manager Adam Bohannon, trade advertising and promotion manager Woody Gilmartin, director of manufacturing Benjamin Lee, and the entire staff at Oxford were as supportive a team as any editor could desire.

The staff of the Mark Twain House provided superb assistance as well. I would like to thank Marianne Curling, curator, Debra Petke, education director, Beverly Zell, curator of photography, Britt Gustafson, assistant director of education, Beth Ann McPherson, assistant curator, and Pam Collins, administrative assistant, for all their generous help, and for allowing us to reproduce books and photographs from the Mark Twain House collection. One could not ask for more congenial or helpful partners in publishing.

G. Thomas Tanselle, vice president of the John Simon Guggenheim Memorial Foundation, and an expert on the history of the book, offered essential advice about how to create as responsible a facsimile edition as possible. I appreciate his very knowledgeable counsel.

I am deeply indebted to Robert H. Hirst, general editor of the Mark Twain Project at The Bancroft Library in Berkeley, for bringing his outstanding knowledge of Twain editions to bear on the selection of the books photographed for the facsimiles, for giving generous assistance all along the way, and for providing his meticulous notes on the text. The set is the richer for his advice. I would also like to express my gratitude to the Mark Twain Project, not only for making texts and photographs from their collection available to us, but also for nurturing Mark Twain studies with a steady infusion of matchless, important publications.

I would like to thank Jeffrey Kaimowitz, curator of the Watkinson Library at Trinity College, Hartford (where the Mark Twain House collection is kept), along with his colleagues Peter Knapp and Alesandra M. Schmidt, for having been instrumental in Robert Hirst's search for first editions that could be safely reproduced. Victor Fischer, Harriet Elinor Smith, and especially Kenneth M. Sanderson, associate editors with the Mark Twain Project, reviewed the note on the text in each volume with cheerful vigilance. Thanks are also due to Mark Twain Project associate editor Michael Frank and administrative assistant Brenda J. Bailey for their help at various stages.

I am grateful to Helen K. Copley for granting permission to publish photographs in the Mark Twain Collection of the James S. Copley Library in La Jolla, California, and to Carol Beales and Ron Vanderhye of the Copley Library for making my research trip to their institution so productive and enjoyable.

Several contributors — David Bradley, Louis J. Budd, Beverly R. David, Robert Hirst, Fred Kaplan, James S. Leonard, Toni Morrison, Lillian S. Robinson, Jeffrey Rubin-Dorsky, Ray Sapirstein, and David L. Smith — were particularly helpful in the early stages of the project, brainstorming about the cast of writers and scholars who could make it work. Others who participated in that process were John Boyer, James Cox, Robert Crunden, Joel Dinerstein, William Goetzmann, Calvin and Maria Johnson, Jim Magnuson, Arnold Rampersad, Siva Vaidhyanathan, Steve and Louise Weinberg, and Richard Yarborough.

Kevin Bochynski, famous among Twain scholars as an "angel" who is gifted at finding methods of making their research run more smoothly, was helpful in more ways than I can count. He did an outstanding job in his official capacity as production consultant to The Oxford Mark Twain, supervising the photography of the facsimiles. I am also grateful to him for having put me in touch via e-mail with Kent Rasmussen, author of the magisterial *Mark Twain A to Z*, who was tremendously helpful as the project proceeded, sharing insights on obscure illustrators and other points, and generously being "on call" for all sorts of unforeseen contingencies.

I am indebted to Siva Vaidhyanathan of the American Studies Program of the University of Texas at Austin for having been such a superb research assistant. It would be hard to imagine The Oxford Mark Twain without the benefit of his insights and energy. A fine scholar and writer in his own right, he was crucial to making this project happen.

Georgia Barnhill, the Andrew W. Mellon Curator of Graphic Arts at the American Antiquarian Society in Worcester, Massachusetts, Tom Staley, director of the Harry Ransom Humanities Research Center at the University of Texas at Austin, and Joan Grant, director of collection services at the Elmer Holmes Bobst Library of New York University, granted us access to their collections and assisted us in the reproduction of several volumes of The Oxford Mark Twain. I would also like to thank Kenneth Craven, Sally Leach, and Richard Oram of the Harry Ransom Humanities Research Center for their help in making HRC materials available, and Jay and John Crowley, of Jay's Publishers Services in Rockland, Massachusetts, for their efforts to photograph the books carefully and attentively.

I would like to express my gratitude for the grant I was awarded by the University Research Institute of the University of Texas at Austin to defray some of the costs of researching The Oxford Mark Twain. I am also grateful to American Studies director Robert Abzug and the University of Texas for the computer that facilitated my work on this project (and to UT systems analyst Steve Alemán, who tried his best to repair the damage when it crashed). Thanks also to American Studies administrative assistant Janice Bradley and graduate coordinator Melanie Livingston for their always generous and thoughtful help.

The Oxford Mark Twain would not have happened without the unstinting, wholehearted support of my husband, Jim Fishkin, who went way beyond the proverbial call of duty more times than I'm sure he cares to remember as he shared me unselfishly with that other man in my life, Mark Twain. I am also grateful to my family — to my sons Joey and Bobby, who cheered me on all along the way, as did Fannie Fishkin, David Fishkin, Gennie Gordon, Mildred Hope Witkin, and Leonard, Gillis, and Moss

Plaine — and to honorary family member Margaret Osborne, who did the same.

My greatest debt is to the man who set all this in motion. Only a figure as rich and complicated as Mark Twain could have sustained such energy and interest on the part of so many people for so long. Never boring, never dull, Mark Twain repays our attention again and again and again. It is a privilege to be able to honor his memory with The Oxford Mark Twain.

Shelley Fisher Fishkin
Austin, Texas
April 1996